MACPHERSON

Sandra Savage

To my dear cousin and constant support in the writing of the Annie Pepper trilogy, Doreen Anderson.

CONTENTS

Chapter 1

"Lexie, Lexie, wait for me!"

The skinny frame of Lexie's younger sibling came panting up behind her.

She glanced down at him. "And why should I wait for you?" she asked, her head tipped to one side and an impatient expression on her face.

Ian MacPherson idolised his stepsister, and with the maturity of a ten-year-old imagined her to be a magical princess.

"No reason!" he replied, hurt at her indifference as always. "Where are you going on Saturday?"

"The electric theatre," she replied airily, "and NO, you can't come."

Ian kicked a stone into the road and dug his hands into his pockets. "Why?"

Lexie stopped walking and turned to face him, her hands firmly planted on her hips and her mouth set. "Because I say so," she replied, "and because I'm going with my friends."

Ian bit his lip. "I'll tell Mum," he retorted, "and she'll make you take me."

Lexie flicked her fair hair over her shoulder and laughed. "Don't care," she called, beginning to run down Forfar Road from the school gate.

Lexie's father had been a police sergeant in the Dundee Constabulary and her mother, Annie Melville, had married Euan MacPherson, also in the police force, after her husband's suicide twelve years ago.

Ian raced past her up the winding stairwell of their tenement home in Stobswell and burst into the front room.

"Mum, Mum," he called breathlessly, "Lexie's going to the electric theatre tomorrow and she's not going to take me. Make her take me Mum, make her take me."

Annie put down her knitting and sighed. "Will you two never stop squabbling?"

Lexie threw down her schoolbooks and flounced onto the settee, crossing her arms defiantly over her chest.

"Just take him, Lexie," Annie asked, "you know he'll just bother the life out of me if you don't."

A wide smile of success spread over Ian's freckled face. But it soon faded.

"NO," came the reply, "I'd rather not go if I've to take him. I'm going with Sarah Dawson and we don't want daft boys along with us.

Annie knew it was an impasse. "Your father will decide," she announced, "when he comes off duty at Bell Street, who's going anywhere."

It was Ian's turn to go into the huff.

Euan MacPherson had adopted Lexie as his own when he married Annie and always had a soft spot for her, despite loving their own son dearly.

"But…" began Ian.

"That's enough," warned Annie. "Now out to play till your tea's ready, and no more arguing."

Lexie grinned. She could twist Euan round her little finger and she knew it.

"You're just like your Auntie Mary used to be," Annie said. "Too high spirited for your own good."

Mary had been Annie's younger sister, who'd died of tuberculosis, leaving her daughter, Nancy, to be brought up by Joe Cassiday, her 'live in' husband and father of their son, little Joe, born a few weeks prior to her death.

"Was Auntie Mary very beautiful?" Lexie asked, not for the first time.

Annie smiled to herself. "She was Lexie," she said wistfully, remembering her sister's sparkle and cleverness. "She had coal-black hair and big brown eyes, and every man in Dundee fell in love with her."

Lexie hugged her knees to her chest and tried to imagine the beautiful woman who'd died so tragically and so young.

"Nancy doesn't really look like her!" Lexie stated thoughtfully. "Does she take after her dad?"

Billy Dawson's face flashed through Annie's mind. It should have been her that married Billy and not Mary, but that was water under the bridge now and she'd gotten over all that pain, although the memory sometimes still brought a tinge of regret.

"She's the spitting image of Joe Cassiday," Annie lied, "just like wee Joe is."

Luckily, both Billy and Joe had dark hair and eyes and Nancy had grown up accepting Joe as her father.

There was a time, after Mary's death and Annie's husband Alex's suicide, when she felt drawn again to Billy, but Josie McIntyre had set her cap at him and it had all been too late. Josie and Billy had married, and had three daughters, the eldest being Sarah Dawson, Lexie's best friend.

Annie shook the memories from her head. "C'mon young woman," she said briskly, "your father will be home soon and expecting his tea and your help's needed in the kitchen."

Lexie followed her mother, knowing when to do as she was told. She'd be leaving school soon and going out to work, if she could find any that is – unemployment was rife in Dundee in 1928, with the jute mills going on short-time and only skilled weavers and spinners managing to hold on to the jobs that remained.

Annie had been lucky that Euan had been in the police force, or life for them would have been just as miserable as the lot of most families in the town. Men hung about street corners, thinking of ways to make money, some legally, some illegally, and betting on 'the horses' was the vice of many.

The Salvation Army, where Annie's sister-in-law and brother-in-law, Isobella and John Anderson commanded high positions, ran soup kitchens and gave life-saving warmth to many a needy soul in the Scottish winters, and Annie herself was often found helping John and Isobella out, in their continual battle to do the Lord's work.

Annie could hear Euan's bootsteps on the stairs, accompanied by the high pitch of Ian's voice as he tried to get into his father's good books before Lexie could use her charms on him to get her own way on Saturday.

"I'll clean your boots for a week," implored Ian, "and go all the messages for Mum…"

Euan hung up his tunic in the hall and called out to Annie.

"What's up wi' this lad, Annie?" he implored, moving through to the kitchen with Ian tagging after him. "What's he after?"

"He wants to go with me to the electric theatre on Saturday," gushed Lexie, "and I'm going with Sarah and, please, please, say he can't come?" She rolled tearful blue eyes in Euan's direction.

"And what's your mother got to say about all this?" he asked, hoping to remain neutral.

"I said," began Annie, emphasising her words, "that you'd decide who goes to what and when."

Euan scraped a chair back from the table and sat down, his eyes going first to one young face and then the other.

"We'll all go," he said decisively. "Your mother and me don't go out often enough and you can sit to one side of us," he indicated to Ian, "and you," now looking at Lexie, "can sit to the other side with Sarah."

He folded his arms across his chest in satisfaction and before any more could be said, picked up the Dundee Courier from the table and began reading.

Annie shrugged her shoulders at her children and began to mash the potatoes. Lexie ate her meal in stony silence. Saturday was going to be a disaster.

Chapter 2

Sarah Dawson opened the door of her home in Morgan Street to find Lexie waiting impatiently.

"You're up early," Sarah said, standing aside to let Lexie enter, "and on a Saturday!"

"Something awful has happened," announced her friend dramatically.

Sarah followed her to the bedroom she shared with her two sisters and closed the door behind her.

Lexie flopped down on Sarah's bed. "Mum and Dad are only coming TONIGHT," she whispered loudly, conscious of Sarah's still-sleeping sisters. "That little brother of mine too, brat that he is."

"But what about...?"

"I know, I know," interrupted Lexie. "We'll just have to get word to them, that's all."

"But, how?"

Lexie waved her hand towards a jotter on the floor by Sarah's bed.

"Robbie works at Harry Duncan's butcher shop on Saturdays, we could slip him a note or something, tell him what's happened."

Sarah was actually quite relieved that the arrangement to meet the two brothers had fallen through. She wasn't as mature as Lexie and hadn't known how to get out of the meeting that Lexie had arranged without her knowledge. She'd agreed to meet Robbie secretly in the darkness of Greens

Electric Theatre in the Nethergate, and that she would bring her friend for his younger brother David.

Sarah tore a page from her jotter and handed it, along with a pencil, to Lexie who began to scribble furiously.

Neither her mother nor father approved of Lexie, although Josie Dawson, who was Lexie's English teacher at school, recognised her quick mind and active imagination as capable of going far, if only her impetuous nature could be harnessed.

Sarah's mother's voice sounded at the bedroom door.

"Sarah," she called, "run down to Mr Guthrie's for some sugar for me." The bedroom door opened.

"Why Lexie!" exclaimed Sarah's mother. "I didn't know you were here."

Lexie jumped up, clutching the note behind her back.

"What's all the noise?" asked a sleepy voice from the bed opposite. Josie hushed her youngest daughter and waited for an explanation.

"I just had to speak to Sarah for a minute," she explained, trying to keep the guilt out of her voice. "Mum and Dad are taking me and Ian to the Greens Theatre tonight and they said I could bring Sarah… if that's alright with you?"

Mrs Dawson frowned. She knew Lexie's mother from before Lexie was born and had always tried not to let her husband's past obsession with Annie colour her judgement of her daughter, but found it difficult.

"I suppose it's alright," she agreed reluctantly, "if you're sure your mother's agreeable."

"Yes, yes, she is," Lexie answered quickly, making for the door. She winked at Sarah as she passed. "I'll see you later then," she said lightly. "The picture starts at six o'clock, it's Charlie Chaplin."

"I'll come over just after tea then," Sarah responded, "see you later."

Josie Dawson sighed. "What is it about the girl that you like so much?" she began, rousing her other daughters while trying to keep the agitation out of her voice. "She's not the type of girl…"

"Please, Mum," interrupted Sarah, "she's *my* friend and she makes me laugh and she's pretty."

Josie held up her hand. "Alright, alright," she said, switching off her 'teacher's voice'. "Just remember your father's position in Dundee and how unhappy he'd be if…"

Josie's voice tailed off. Since Billy had been elected as Town Councillor for the district of Maryfield, they had been thrown into public life, and Josie was more conscious than ever of being the wife of a prominent man with all that involved.

"I'm thirteen," Sarah reminded Josie, her smock barely concealing the shapeliness which was forming underneath it, "and I'm a good girl."

Josie smiled, reassured of her daughter's innocence. "C'mon," she said, "fetch that sugar and we'll say no more about it."

Sarah breathed a sigh of relief and set off to Mr Guthrie's shop. It was difficult being the daughter of the teacher, always having to set an example and now, as well as that, the daughter of a town councillor. Lexie, in comparison to her, seemed to have such a free and easy life, her stepfather always giving in to her demands and her mother happy to let him do so.

But just the same, she was glad she didn't have to go through with the dreaded meeting. Boys were something seen from afar only and, according to her mother, should not be of interest to nice young girls.

Lexie looked at the clock tower of Morgan School. It was only half past eight, plenty of time. Clutching the note tightly in her hand, she made her way down Albert Street and Princes Street and into King Street, where Harry Duncan had his butcher's shop.

Huge sides of beef streaked with yellow fat hung on hooks from a rail by the door and the window was laid out with links of sausages and trays of mince, liver and kidneys, and a mini mountain of tripe.

She peered into the gloom, hoping to catch the eye of Robbie Robertson but only the back of Harry Duncan, stripping bones with his flashing knife, was visible.

She'd have to go in.

She smoothed the front of her smock and edged her toes through the door and onto the sawdust covered floor.

Mr Duncan continued with his task. Lexie edged in further. Through a door at the back of the shop, she could just see movement and coughed gently, in an endeavour to attract the attention of Robbie. The butcher turned at the sound and came towards her, the bloodied knife still in his hand.

Lexie felt herself colour under his gaze and gulped.

"Well," Harry Duncan continued, "an' what can I get you?"

"Nnnn… Nothing," Lexie replied quickly, her courage deserting her, "I was just looking."

She turned quickly to make her exit, running into a side of beef as she did so.

"Careful," called out the butcher, shaking his head before turning back to his task. "Youngsters," he muttered.

Robbie Robertson saw Lexie and her predicament from the darkness of the back shop.

"Mr Duncan," he called through, "I'll just tak' these bones oot back fir the bone man to pick up later on."

Harry Duncan nodded his assent and Robbie quickly manoeuvred the galvanised bin of bones towards the back door. Once outside he raced up the flight of stairs leading into Todburn Lane and ran towards its junction with Dens Brae hoping to catch Lexie on her flight back up King Street.

He'd just turned into Dens Brae as she went hurrying past.

"Lexie," he called loudly, "wait."

Lexie couldn't believe her luck. "Robbie." She waved. "I've been trying to get a message to you."

Robbie ran up to her, his eyes gleaming with delight at seeing her.

"Well, what's the message?" he asked, breathing heavily from the running.

Lexie hung her head. "I can't meet you tonight," she said with the torment of the young in love. "My mum and dad are coming to the Greens and so is Ian and it's all just AWFUL."

She could feel tears of disappointment sting the corners of her eyes.

"Oh," Robbie replied, his shoulders visibly drooping. He was a big lad for his sixteen years and had worked for Harry Duncan since he was fourteen, his muscles benefiting both from the heavy lifting and the extra meat he got on Saturday. He'd lived with his mother and brother in an attic room on Victoria Road since his father had been killed in the Great War and had gone to work as soon as he'd been old enough.

"Maybe you could meet us on Sunday instead," he suggested ardently, "just like we'd planned for tonight, but at the park instead?"

Lexie brightened and blushed. "I suppose me and Sarah could just run into you and Davie at Baxters Park, accidentally, of course."

Robbie grinned widely.

"Sunday it is then," he said eagerly, "now I'd best get back to the shop, Mr Duncan'll be wonderin' where I am."

They gazed at one another in mutual admiration for a moment, before

Robbie waved goodbye and hurried back up Dens Brae and into Todburn Lane, turning as he did so to blow Lexie a kiss.

She felt very grown up. Sunday would be wonderful.

Chapter 3

"Wake up Nancy you'll be late for your work."

The anxious voice of her stepmother, Agnes Cassiday, barged uninvited into Nancy's dream.

"You've slept in again."

Nancy forced her weary eyes open. She hated working at the mill, but most of all she hated working on Saturday. She could hear Agnes raking the coals of last night's fire, trying to rekindle some life back into it and flopped back onto her pillow.

Her younger brothers, Joe, Sean and Michael stirred in their slumber.

"Are you gettin' up?" Agnes's voice was becoming impatient. Nancy was seventeen years of age and should be married with children of her own, not still taking up space in the cramped two roomed tenement house in William Lane, which was their home.

Nancy pushed herself up to a sitting position with her elbow and rubbed her eyes. At least it was only a half day on Saturday. Nancy was a good weaver, like her Auntie Annie had been before her and it was only the skilled and fit who had held on to their jobs, now that the orders for jute cloth were drying up. The fact that her real father, Billy Dawson, was also the mill manager may also have helped, but as far as Nancy was concerned, he was a name only. Joe Cassiday was the one she called dad.

She walked slowly through into the kitchen, which also served as a living room and dining room, not to mention a bedroom for Joe and Agnes, and splashed cold water on her face from the cold tap beneath the small window.

Agnes was stirring porridge on the gas cooker for her breakfast.

"Here," she said, tipping the hot oatmeal into a shallow bowl, "hurry up an' eat this afore you go or you'll be faintin' at your looms."

Nancy pulled her smock over her head and tied it at the back.

"I'll not faint," she answered back shortly, ignoring the offering. "You eat it, you look as if you could do with it."

Agnes flinched. Nancy had never taken to her and was always vying for Joe's attention, stirring up trouble for her, it seemed, any chance she could. She looked at her scrawny hands holding the pot and spirtle, age spots, brown and numerous, interspersed with chilblains and purple veins looked back at her.

She'd been bonnie once, she told herself, when she'd first met Joe and fallen for his Irish charms. But the strains of a difficult pregnancy with the twins and working to support her husband and mixed brood had taken their toll.

"Please yourself." She shrugged, turning away to disguise the hurt she felt. Nancy was a beauty and she knew it. Jet black curls and huge brown eyes fought for supremacy over her other, equally attractive features, and her neat five foot two inch frame made men feel they could sweep her up and carry her off in their arms. Many wanted to, but only one had succeeded. Billy Donnelly.

She drank down a cup of water and cut a thick slice of bread from the loaf on the board. "This'll do me," she said, spooning on a blob of jam before disappearing out the door. "Cheerio Dad," she called over her shoulder, "sing one for me tonight."

Agnes sighed and began spooning the porridge into her mouth.

"Sing one fir me the night an' all," she muttered, "an' try no' to drink all the takings afore you come home."

Joe hadn't worked a day since the Great War, when he'd been invalided out as an amputee. Mary's love had saved him from going under then, but when she had died, leaving him alone to look after Nancy and little Joe, desperation had drawn him to Agnes.

She was never the love of his life, but he was the love of hers and over the years she had silently borne the brunt of his subsequent bouts of depression and drunkenness.

"Was that Nancy's voice I heard?" he muttered gruffly.

Joe rolled over in the double bed in the alcove and scratched the stubble on his chin.

Agnes nodded in reply.

Joe swung his leg over the side of the bed and pulled the stump of the other alongside it.

"Pass me the gammy one," he instructed Agnes, "unless you want to see me falling over sober as well as drunk."

Agnes pushed the tin leg towards him. "I suppose you'll be singin' the night?"

Joe strapped on the appendage and hoisted himself to a standing position. First thing in the morning was always the worst as gravity pulled the blood into the stump and he winced.

"So what if I am?" he retorted through gritted teeth. "You're not going to deny me every pleasure in this life."

Agnes frowned. "I wouldna' deny you onythin' Joe," she said truthfully, "I just worry aboot you, drinkin' so much, that's all."

"Well stop worrying and pour me some tea."

He drank it in silence while the pain in his leg subsided.

"Tonight's going to be special," he said, when he'd drained the cup and handed it back to Agnes for a refill. "George Grant from Grant's Concert Party's coming in to hear me sing and if he likes what he hears… well, who knows."

Agnes felt her spirits lift for the first time in a long time.

"Do you mean you could sing on the stage… for REAL money?"

Joe smiled a smile that almost broke Agnes's heart with its wistfulness.

"Aye Agnes," he said softly, "singing for his supper."

She'd never seen Joe look so happy, radiant almost. "That would be braw," she whispered, suddenly aware of the significance of what her husband was saying. "We'll keep our fingers crossed, Joe, me an' the laddies."

"And Nancy," he added, "don't forget Nancy."

The good feeling drained from Agnes's heart. "No Joe," she replied, "I'll no' forget her."

The weavers were gathered at the mill gate, breathing their last gulps of fresh air before entering into the weaving flat with its haze of dust and jute fibres.

"We're gain' to the Progress Hall the night Nancy, are you comin'?"

Nancy flashed her dark eyes at her fellow millworkers. "Of course," she replied, "I wouldn't miss Saturday night dancin' at the Proggie for anything or anybody."

"No' even Billy Donnelly," giggled Mary Morrison, covering her mouth with her rough little hand to hide the gaps in her teeth.

Nancy felt a rush of colour to her face at the mention of Billy's name.

"And what do you know about me and Billy Donnelly?" she asked quickly, worried that word of her association with the spinner from Cox's Mill in Lochee would reach Joe's ears and he'd put a stop to it, like he'd done to anyone who'd paid any attention to her in the past.

"Nothin," squealed Mary, rushing ahead of them to get into the weaving flat before Nancy could say any more. The sound of the seven o'clock bummer ended the speculation.

"See you at the Proggie the night then Nancy?"

Nancy acknowledged the invitation of her peers with a smile. "Yes, see you tonight."

The looms whined into life and their clattering filled the air with a wall of noise, preventing any further conversation between the mill lassies. Nancy's fingers tied off the ends of jute with speed and precision as her eyes watched the shuttles whiz back and forth between the yarn, forming the rough hessian cloth, but her mind was elsewhere. Pictures of Billy Donnelly, all six feet of him, lean and hungry for anything the world could put his way, flashed into her mind's eye. He was as Irish as Joe and, like him, had come over from Ireland with his mammy and daddy to find a better life, but they'd settled in the west end of Dundee in an area that the locals had nicknamed 'Tipperary'.

They'd first met at the Progress Halls, situated as it was on the steep slope of the Hilltown a few weeks back, when Billy had danced her off her feet. She could almost hear the music above the racket of the looms and feel his strong arm circling her waist, whirling her round and round and tonight, she'd see him again for sure.

Chapter 4

"I'm worried about that girl," announced Josie as Sarah left for her evening at Greens Electric Theatre with Lexie and her family.

Billy folded his newspaper and paid attention. "Why?" he asked, hoping the conversation wouldn't swing round to Lexie's mother, Annie Melville.

"She's thirteen now," continued Josie, "and getting to that age... you know!"

Billy lit a cigarette and waited. "And," he said, "what do I know?"

"Well, you know we want her to get a good education and maybe go into teaching and..."

Billy blew the cigarette smoke into the air. "And?" he said again, this time with an edge of impatience creeping into his voice.

"And I don't like the influence that Lexie Melville's having on her." The words came out more hurried and anxious than she'd wanted, but at last they were out.

Billy felt the muscles in his shoulders tighten. "And what influence is this then?"

"Well..." Josie went on, "you know..." Her eyes found a spot on the carpet and fixed there.

"Do I?" Billy asked, knowing where the question was leading.

Josie took a deep breath. Even after all these years, the thought of Annie Melville and Billy's love for her still rankled. "Like mother, like daughter, I suppose," she said curtly.

Billy knew of old not to be drawn into a discussi
been obsessed with love for her in the old days, I
instead and Annie had married Euan MacPherson a
the past, except in Josie's mind.

"Don't you think you're being a bit unfair on Lexie?" Billy said soft,
"She's only a young girl finding her feet."

Fingers of jealousy wound round Josie's heart. "She may be a young girl,
Billy Dawson, but she's forward and reckless and she'll come to no good
and I don't want out daughter associating with her."

Billy knew there was no talking to Josie when she was in an 'Annie
Melville' mood.

"And what do you want me to do about it?" Billy asked, not really
wishing to know.

"Forbid her to see Lexie Melville," she said emphatically. "You're her
father, forbid her, before it's too late."

"Josie," Billy began, aware it was the mother and not the child who was
getting to his wife, "isn't that a bit harsh on the girl? After all, she's done
nothing to warrant your dislike of her and…"

Josie sprang to her feet. "There you go, defending the indefensible," she
wailed. "I'm telling you she's a bad influence."

"Alright, alright," Billy rounded, his patience dissolving into anger, "I'll
speak to Sarah, but I'm not going to forbid her doing anything. She's old
enough to understand what's right and what's wrong and if she's not, then
we've not taught her very well, despite your abilities in the classroom."

The remark stung Josie to the quick. She was a good teacher and a good
mother and her only concern was her daughter's future, couldn't Billy see
that?

The rest of the evening passed in silence as each of them searched for
reasons to speak again without loss of face. But they found none and it was
an uneasy silence which greeted Sarah on her return from Greens Theatre.

She rushed in, her face flushed with excitement.

"It was wonderful," she gushed, "Charlie Chaplin is the funniest little
man you've ever seen, ever."

She threw her coat over the back of a chair and flopped down into it.
Her two younger sisters sat side by side on the sofa, their faces masked by a
book which they were hiding behind rather than reading.

ıme you two were in bed," Billy said to them. "Your mother and I ıt to speak to Sarah."

The youngsters obediently slid from the sofa and left the room, casting wide-eyed glances at their sister as they passed her.

The delight which had been evident in Sarah's eyes, faded.

"What's wrong?" she asked, her mind racing to conclude that somehow her mother and father had found out about the original reason she was going to the picture show with Lexie.

"I'll make some tea," Josie said, standing up, "let me know when to bring it through."

Billy nodded towards the sofa and Sarah sat. She was glad it was just her and her father. She could speak to him and he'd listen, not like her mother.

"You're very fond of Lexie, aren't you?" Billy asked evenly, as they both sat down, "and I'm sure she's very fond of you too."

Sarah nodded.

"Thing is, Sarah," Billy went on, lighting a cigarette to buy himself some time to form the words he didn't want to say, "your mother...and me, we're not sure Lexie Melville's the most suitable company for you."

Sarah was almost certain now that her father had found out about Robbie and Davie Robertson, but her nerve held.

"She's nice," Sarah stated, "and she makes me laugh, especially when I get worried about exams and stuff... don't you like her?"

His daughter's candid statement and question required an honest response.

"Of course I like her," Billy answered truthfully. How could he not like the daughter of Annie Melville? He pushed the admission from his mind.

"But it's not a question of like, Sarah, it's more what's best for you and your future."

Sarah frowned. "It's Mum, isn't it," she said, suddenly realising it had nothing to do with the boys. "She doesn't like Lexie and she doesn't like her coming round here."

Billy nodded in resignation. He could no more forbid his daughter from seeing her friend than he could forbid himself breathing.

"Go to bed Sarah," he sighed, "and just remember your mother's counting on you to do well at school and..."

"Become a teacher," Sarah concluded, "like her."

Billy smiled at his daughter. "Something like that," he said, satisfied that she had sufficient common sense to deal with anything Lexie Melville could lead her into. But Billy was wrong.

Tomorrow, Lexie and her were meeting Robbie and Davie Robertson in Baxter's Park. Lexie had arranged it all, of course, and had whispered the news to Sarah as they left the picture house. Sarah was not looking forward to the rendezvous.

Chapter 5

The lights of the Progress Halls in the Hilltown shone into the night as Nancy and Lizzie Green, joined the throng of Saturday night dancers ascending the steep brae, drawn to the lights like moths to a flame.

Lizzie was a young weaver, like Nancy, and they'd worked alongside one another for the past two years in Baxter's Mill. Lizzie was as Scottish as Nancy was Irish, but the two girls shared everything, clothes, money, food, secrets and confidences.

"Do you think he'll be here?" asked Lizzie, inhaling deeply as the steep climb began to affect her breathing.

"Who?"

Lizzie gurgled. "Who! *Billy Donnelly*, of course."

Nancy smiled enigmatically. "Maybe."

Lizzie tossed her head. "Don't kid me on your no' botherin'."

"Maybe I am," Nancy replied, maintaining her mysterious smile, "but then again, maybe I'm not."

They joined the queue jostling to gain entry to the lights and music, with Lizzie shaking her head and giving up her attempt to prise any snippets of information from Nancy.

"Two please," said Nancy, handing over two shillings.

The cashier glanced briefly at the girls and handed them their tickets.

The sound of music filled their ears and mixed with the exited chatter of

18

the crowd. Nancy glanced casually around the hall, willing Billy Donnelly to be there.

"Well," nudged Lizzie, "is 'e here?"

"I told you Lizzie Green," Nancy responded coyly, "maybe he's coming and maybe he's not."

"Nancy Cassiday!" exclaimed Lizzie, laughing, "your no' very good at tellin' lies."

It was Lizzie who saw him first.

"No' that your botherin', of course," she whispered, "but you might wish to ken that Mr Donnelly's just walked in."

Nancy felt her heart leap in her breast, as she forced her eyes not to follow Lizzie's pointing finger.

"Is he looking this way Lizzie?" she hissed, suddenly forgetting her act of indifference.

Lizzie squeezed her arm. "Not only is he lookin' this way... *he's comin' over.*"

Nancy's heart beat even faster and her tongue suddenly felt welded to the roof of her mouth. A surge of adrenalin had turned her legs to jelly and for a moment she thought she would faint.

The strong hand of Billy Donnelly gripped her elbow.

"Would you be for dancin' Nancy?" he asked, his soft Irish brogue pouring over her like warm honey.

"I would," she answered demurely, unable to meet his eyes, just yet.

"Do you mind, Lizzie?" he asked. Lizzie shook her head.

"No bother Billy," she said, smiling knowingly at Nancy.

Billy led Nancy onto the dance floor, and to the strains of Alex McAvoy's Accordion Band, they moved as one to a slow foxtrot.

Neither spoke till the dance was over, but with every passing minute, Nancy was falling more and more under Billy's spell.

"Will you dance with me again?" he asked, returning her to the waiting Lizzie.

Nancy nodded. "I will," she said, "and... thank you."

"Thank *you*," smiled Billy, his dark eyes seeming to hypnotise her, as he took his leave.

"WELL!" Lizzie squealed.

Nancy turned to her friend. "Do you believe in love?" she whispered dreamily. "Real love, I mean."

Lizzie nodded vigorously.

"Then you're looking at… a woman in love."

Lizzie eyes widened. "An' does he love you too, Nancy?"

The enigmatic smile had returned. "I think so, Lizzie," she breathed, "I think so."

The rest of the evening passed in a flurry of sound and movement for the two girls, till Alex McAvoy announced the last waltz.

"Take your partners," he drawled suggestively, "fir the last dance."

The heat was oppressive now, as Nancy and Lizzie waited to be asked.

Johnny Patterson, a batcher in the lower mill, pounced on Lizzie. He'd been eyeing her all night but had only now, plucked up the courage to ask her to dance. Nancy was left alone. For what seemed like forever, she stood, hardly daring to breathe and trying not to search out Billy's face amongst the crowd.

The music played on and Nancy felt a stab of disappointment pierce her heart.

It was the last dance but Billy was nowhere to be seen.

By the time Lizzie with Johnny in tow had found her again, she was almost in tears.

"C'mon," she whispered, "let's go home."

Lizzie didn't have to ask what was wrong, Billy's absence already told her.

"Men," she muttered, ushering Nancy towards the door.

A pair of strong hands stopped Nancy in her flight.

"You're not going already?" asked Billy Donnelly anxiously.

Nancy looked up into the dark eyes, made even darker with worry.

"The dance is over," replied Nancy, "but obviously you haven't noticed."

Billy looked heavenward. "I'm sorry," he said, as the crowd of dancers pushed past them towards the exit, "two of the boys from Cox's had too much to drink and were spoiling for a fight. If I hadn't stayed with them, they'd be in the infirmary by now… or worse."

Nancy felt herself relax. He hadn't forgotten her after all.

"Can I speak with you… for a minute… please?" he said, still holding her arms with his hands.

Nancy looked at Lizzie.

"Don't mind me," her friend assured her, "Johnny'll see I get home alright."

Nancy allowed Billy to manoeuvre her through the crowd and out into the night air.

"Will you let me walk you home?" he asked.

Nancy nodded. "I'd like that."

Seamlessly and in step, they made their way down the Hilltown and into Victoria Road.

"Where do you live?" Billy asked, taking her hand in his.

"Not far," Nancy answered, "William Lane."

It wasn't till they were nearly at the close entrance that Nancy saw Joe, smoking a cigarette, the gas lamp in the lane casting a long shadow across the cassies.

"It's my dad," she whispered fearfully to Billy, suddenly coming down from her pink cloud into the harsh reality of her predicament.

Joe had always insisted to Agnes that his protectiveness towards his stepdaughter was purely to prevent her being hurt, but it was more than that, Joe was jealous of anyone who took Nancy's attention away from him. But in Billy Donnelly, he was to meet his match.

"Dad," Nancy called out softly, trying to keep any anxiety out of her voice, "I didn't expect to see you here."

Joe inhaled on his cigarette and flicked it into the night air, a shower of sparks showing where it had landed.

"That's obvious."

Billy's grip tightened round Nancy's hand. "Donnelly's the name," he said amiably, "Billy Donnelly."

"Is it now?" Joe responded tensely. "Well, well, well."

"I was just seeing your daughter safely home, Mr Cassiday."

Joe lit another cigarette as another surge of jealousy coursed through him. Nancy may be his stepdaughter, but she was no blood relation to him and she was as tempting to him as she was to any other red-blooded male, Billy Donnelly being one of them.

Joe's eyes squinted into the darkness as he tried to discern Billy's features. He could see he was tall and strong with *both* feet firmly planted on the ground. Silently, Joe cursed his gammy leg. If it wasn't for that…

"Well, you've seen her safely home," he said icily, "don't let me keep you."

Both men stared at one another, Billy confused and Joe determined.

"Dad!" Nancy exclaimed. "It was very kind of Billy to see me home…"

"KIND," Joe exploded, unable to keep the green-eyed monster under control any longer. "I know why he's here," he spat, "and so does HE." Joe pulled Nancy towards him. "But unlucky for him, *I* was waiting."

But Billy held his ground. "You're wrong, Mr Cassiday, I have every respect for your daughter."

Joe pushed Nancy further behind him. "RESPECT," he echoed, "and where did an Irish layabout like you learn respect?"

By now, windows were being opened and sleepy heads appeared, wondering what all the shouting was about.

"Hud yir tongue," called out a weary voice from the top landing, "there's folk up here tryin' to sleep."

Joe glared at Billy. "On your way, Mr Donnelly," he hissed, "and if you've got any sense, you'll not come back."

Billy felt hot anger flow into his fists. "Oh, I'll be back, Mr Cassiday," he retorted, through clenched teeth, "you have my word on it."

Nancy felt herself dissolve into despair. Why did Joe always do this to her?

"Goodnight, Nancy," called Billy, stepping back of the pavement into the lane, "I'll be in touch."

Joe pulled Nancy roughly behind him, muttering all the while to himself.

"Stop it," Nancy begged, "stop it, you're hurting me."

"And you're hurting ME!" Joe replied, tears of reaction welling up in his eyes as he released his grip on his stepdaughter.

"I was waiting to tell you my news," he said, his voice now a whisper, "and you've spoiled it."

Nancy could hear him sniffing as he fought to control the wave of emotion that was getting out of control.

"I'm sorry," she said, scared at the intensity of Joe's reaction to Billy, "I didn't mean to spoil your news."

Joe raised his head, his eyes bleak and wounded. "Christ, you're beautiful," he murmured, almost reverently.

Nancy's flinched. For a long time now, since she'd turned fifteen, she'd been aware of Joe's affectionate behaviour towards her, even using it to her advantage at times and her dislike of Agnes had fostered her encouragement of him, but this was different, this was no longer a game to annoy her stepmother and Nancy was afraid.

"What's your news then?" she asked, trying to keep her voice light, although her heart was heavy.

"Your old man Joe's going to be a professional singer," he announced, regaining his equilibrium and recapturing the euphoria he'd felt when George Grant had offered him a guinea a night to sing at the Black Watch Club.

Nancy clutched her hands together. "But that's wonderful," she cried, "what did Agnes say when you told her?"

Joe's eyes flashed fire at her. "I haven't told her yet," he said harshly, "I wanted *you* to be the first to know."

Nancy felt herself boxed into a corner. There was no mistaking Joe's intentions now.

"Just think, Nancy," he continued, excitement creeping into his voice, "up there on the stage, being paid to sing." He grasped her arms with his hands. "Will you come to see me singing, Nancy?" he asked. "Say you will."

Nancy felt herself draw back. "It's not me who you should be saying this to," she said quietly. "It's Agnes, your wife, you should be asking."

Joe released his grip on her arms and gazed up at the moon through the roofs and chimneys of the tenement homes which surrounded them, suddenly dejected again.

"Leave me," he said grimly, "go tell Agnes the news. I'm for staying out for a while longer."

Nancy took her chance and escaped into the house.

Agnes was sitting by the fire, rocking backwards and forwards in her chair, tears glistening in the glow of the coals.

"You don't ha'e to tell me," she said, keeping her eyes fixed on the burning flames, "I heard him, along wi' the rest of the land."

Nancy felt a rush of pity for her stepmother and remorse at the way she'd ridiculed her in the past. She'd been foolish and wicked and now she was paying for it. She didn't want Joe, she never had, it had all been a silly game, with Agnes the butt of the joke, but now she wanted Billy Donnelly, more than anything else in the world and she knew she needed Agnes on her side, if she was to get him.

Chapter 6

"But what'll I say to him?" squealed Sarah for the umpteenth time, as Lexie dragged her impatiently towards Baxters Park.

"*Anything.*"

Sarah wrenched her arm free of Lexie's grip. "I can't do it," she said, tears of guilt and confusion welling in her eyes. "What if Mum finds out... or worse still... DAD."

Lexie rolled her eyes heavenward.

"For goodness sake," she said, failing to disguise her annoyance, "we're only going for a walk in the park."

Sarah's mouth set in a frown. "No we're not," she said huffily, "we're going to meet boys."

"Alright, alright," Lexie agreed, "but we're only going to walk round the park and talk a bit..."

"There, you see." The tremor was back in Sarah's voice. "I don't know what to talk about."

Lexie sighed and put her arm around her friend's shoulder. They may not be far apart in years, but in confidence and daring, Lexie was miles in front.

"Look, leave the talking to me and just smile." Lexie flashed a winsome grin. "See?"

The park was big and empty and the trees rustled at them as they passed.

Sarah's feet felt as though they were weighted down with seven-league boots as every step took her nearer to her terror.

"There they are," whispered Lexie, waving to the two distant figures. "C'mon, let's run."

The exertion of running, coupled with Sarah's shallow breathing, sent her heart racing. "Stop, please," she gasped, "I'm getting a stitch."

But Lexie didn't stop and Sarah, breathing heavily, watched her disappear out of sight as the path took a turn behind a huge rhododendron bush.

For a moment, all Sarah could hear was the thumping of her heart and the air rushing in and out of her nose, then she heard Lexie squeal and giggle.

She looked around her. There was no one in sight, not even the park keeper and the late afternoon sky was turning into twilight.

All her mother's words about Lexie flooded into her head. How could she explain being in the park with Lexie and two boys to her!

The head of Davie Robertson appeared around the side of the bush and Sarah felt herself freeze to the spot. Davie was smaller than his brother, much smaller, and looked as though he needed a good scrub. His hair stood in spikes on his head and his dangling arms hung from the rolled up sleeves of a woollen jumper.

She watched, with ever-widening eyes, as Davie licked his hand and slapped it down onto his spiky hair, but to no avail.

He thrust his hands into his pockets and strolled towards her, then round her, before stopping in front of her.

"Are you Sarah?" he asked, grinning through gaps in his teeth.

Sarah managed to nod.

He looked over his shoulder and nodded towards the rhododendron. "Rab says we've no' to bother him an' Lexie just now. No' till he'z kissed 'er anyway."

Sarah felt herself recoil in horror.

"Kissed her," she squeaked, her brain suddenly grasping the implication of what Davie Robertson was saying and what Lexie was doing!

She started to back away, shaking her head as she did so. "My mother's expecting me home," she blurted out, before turning and running full pelt in the direction of the park gate.

Davie Robertson may have been small but he was a fast runner and, to her horror, she could hear him pounding behind her… and GAINING.

She could feel her chin quiver with fear as her legs refused to go any faster.

"Dinna run away!" shouted Davie, catching the back of her smock and reining her in like a horse.

"Let GO!" Sarah screamed. "I want to go home." But Davie wasn't for letting go and he wrestled her to the ground, pinning her arms over her head and laying the weight of his body on top of her.

Sarah had never felt so scared. She could feel Davie's hot breath on her face as droplets of saliva fell from his lips, splattering her with their wetness.

From somewhere inside her, she seemed to get an extra reserve of strength and managed to push Davie off her and onto his back. Scrambling and stumbling she reached the park gate and, never looking back, ran wildly into Pitkerro Road and didn't stop till the darkness of her close, swallowed her up.

She flopped down on the stone steps, breathing heavily and fighting to contain great sobs of reaction which surged from the pit of her stomach. She couldn't go into the house in this state, her mother would surely know something was wrong and it was only the opening of a neighbour's door an hour later, which forced her to make the decision to go up the stairs to the house.

Luckily, her mother was busy helping Jane and Elizabeth with their homework and only acknowledged her daughter's presence, announcing she was home, with a single instruction, before returning to the task in hand. "Put the kettle on."

Sarah went into the kitchen and filled the kettle from the cold tap. Hardly daring to look, she glanced at her reflection in her father's shaving mirror, balanced on the window ledge.

Her eyes were still huge and shining with moistness, but apart from that, she looked more or less her usual self. She took a deep breath and vowed, silently, that she'd never speak to Lexie Melville again, do everything her mother told her, and never, never, go near boys ever, ever again. Having made the vow, she felt a bit better.

"Kettle's on," she called through the half-open door of the front room, "I'm going to bed to read. See you in the morning."

Josie glanced at the clock, it was only seven thirty, but deciding that Sarah must be feeling tired after her late night at Greens Theatre on the Saturday, made no comment. "Goodnight dear," she called back, "sleep well."

Alone in the bedroom, Sarah tried to unscramble her thoughts. How could Lexie let a boy *kiss* her… but worse than that, expect Sarah, her *best friend*, to do the same thing with the obnoxious Davie? Sarah shuddered at the memory.

But she was home now, home and safe, and she redoubled her intention *never* to speak to Lexie Melville again.

She untied her white smock and pulled it from her shoulders, as she prepared for bed. To her horror, bright green grass stains, acquired during her wrestling match with Davie Robertson were streaked across the back. Sarah stared at the evidence of her deceit.

There was no way she could explain THIS to her mother. In a panic, she pushed the offending garment under the mattress of her bed. Somehow, she would have to get rid of the smock before either her mother or father, or her sisters for that matter, saw it. But how? Where?

Sarah's dilemma was far from over. She could feel tears returning to her dry eyes.

"Lexie Melville," she fumed into the darkness, "it's all your fault."

Not even the return of a disgruntled Davie to his brother's side, with the news that Sarah had 'run awa' hame' could ruin the moment for Robbie and Lexie.

"Then you'll just ha'e to 'run awa' hame' yoursel', Davie," replied his brother, his eyes never leaving Lexie's. "Me an' Lexie have things to discuss."

Davie swore under his breath. "Are you no' comin' too?" he asked, reverting back to being Robbie's little brother again. "It's a long walk to the Vici Road?"

Robbie tore his eyes away from Lexie's but kept his arm firmly wrapped around her waist. "NO," stated Robbie emphatically. The look said it all and Davie departed, muttering and kicking the grass as he went.

It was dark now and the park was taking on the shadows of night as Robbie and Lexie walked along the winding paths and around the flower beds, pausing now and then to indulge in a passionate kiss.

"Oh, Robbie," breathed Lexie, after each exchange, "you're wonderful." Which invariably resulted in a further demonstration of Robbie's expertise as a 'kisser'.

Lexie wished her friends, and especially Sarah, could see how grown up she was. She was sure none of them had kissed a boy before and wondered vaguely why Sarah had run away from Davie. She couldn't wait to tell her all about her romantic evening with Robbie. But that would have to wait, tonight was for her and Robbie.

It was gone nine o'clock before Lexie got home, just as Annie and Euan were beginning to worry about their wilful daughter.

"What time do you call this?" began Euan, as Nancy popped her head round the door of the front room. Lexie affected her 'little girl' voice.

"Sorry, Dad," she mewed, "I was at Sarah's and forgot the time. SORRY."

Euan sighed. "Have you no control over that girl, Annie?" he asked. "She seems to do just what she wants."

"Oh, she'll soon be working," Annie replied, patiently, "then married to some unsuspecting laddie, I suppose. That'll soon clip her wings, just like it did her Auntie Mary's."

Euan accepted the response with a resigned sniff. "Well, just keep an eye on her, that's all," he said, "we don't want anything... happening!"

"She may be forward, Euan," smiled Annie, "but she's a good girl underneath. I'm sure she wouldn't do anything to bring shame on herself, or us for that matter."

Annie was right, Lexie was a good girl, but right now, she was in love with Robbie Robertson.

Chapter 7

"Would you like me to make you some tea?" Nancy asked tentatively. Agnes continued to stare at the glowing coals and shook her head.

"You must be pleased for Joe," Nancy continued, trying to bridge the enormous gulf she had dug between herself and her stepmother.

"What difference does it make, whither I'm pleased or no'?" she asked. "An' since when did *you* care, Nancy Cassiday?"

Nancy flinched for she knew she didn't care, not really, she just wanted Joe off her back so she could be with Billy Donnelly and she was using Agnes, as usual.

"Well, sorry I spoke," Nancy retorted, aware that she wasn't fooling Agnes for one minute. "It's just that Joe'll be wanting you to go and see him sing and…"

The look in Agnes's eyes stopped Nancy in her tracks.

"Will 'e now?" she said, gathering her bitterness at Nancy's closeness to her husband. "Now I wonder how tha' is, considerin' he's already asked you?"

Nancy folded her arms defensively. "Only because he saw me first!" she stated. She'd underestimated Agnes's powers of observation and her resentment towards her.

Agnes stood up and straightened her back. "What's up Nancy?" she smiled bitterly, "Suddenly fed up o' auld Joe, are you, somebody younger come along maybe?"

Agnes was too close to the mark for comfort and Nancy felt like she could see right through her.

"Don't think fir one minute," Agnes continued, leaning closer to Nancy's face, "that either you or Joe have been foolin' me these last two years and don't think I'll jump to your tune, Miss Cassiday, just 'cause it suits your needs now."

Nancy stepped back. The woman who had been the brunt of her scorn now seemed to grow in stature before her eyes, and any hopes she'd harboured of offloading Joe back onto his wife were rapidly vanishing.

"I'm sure I don't know what you're talking about," Nancy managed to say through the cloud of butterflies which had suddenly invaded her stomach. "Joe's been very good to me since my mother died and I appreciate it, that's all."

The sound of Joe's footsteps in the small lobby quickly ended the conversation.

"Still up?" he asked both women simultaneously, sensing the tension in the air.

"Just going to bed now," said Nancy quickly, hurrying through to the back room, unwilling to become involved in any further conversation with Joe.

He sat down in the chair opposite his wife and narrowed his eyes menacingly.

"What've you been sayin' to Nancy?"

Agnes felt her lips tighten with hurt at the harshness of Joe's voice.

"Nuthin'"

Joe sat slowly back into his chair.

"And make sure you keep it that way," he said, arousing deeper pain in his wife.

Agnes screwed up every ounce of her courage. "An' if I don't?"

The silence could almost be felt as Joe, once more, leaned towards her.

"I'll kill you."

Agnes felt a wave of shock hit her. "You lov' 'er that much, do you Joe?" she whispered, her heart breaking with each word.

Joe lifted his head and fixed his gaze at the door through to the back room.

"That's none of your business," he said curtly, "now get out of my sight before you say something you'll regret."

The years of struggling against poverty and Joe's drinking had taken their toll on Agnes and, where once there had been a strong spirit, now there was barely a spark of self-esteem. She'd hoped and prayed that the lust she'd seen in her husband's eyes when Nancy was around would, somehow, fade with time, but there was no fooling herself now and the last vestiges of self-respect died within her as she crawled between the blankets of their bed, pulling them over her head to hide the sounds of her pain.

Nancy lay in the darkness in the adjoining room, her eyes wide open, listening to the low rumble of Joe's voice and Agnes's whimpering. Her half brother, little Joe and the twin sons who were her stepbrothers, Sean and Michael, snuffled and sighed as they fought one another, in their sleep, for space in their shared bed.

It was clear that Agnes was going to be of no help to her in her efforts to escape Joe's attentions and, if anything, their encounter seemed to have somehow brought Agnes's bitter emotions to the surface. Nancy could feel her frustrations building inside her and pulled the covers up round her neck, forcing her eyes shut as she did so, in an effort to blot out the despair which was beginning to invade her heart.

She heard Joe get into bed and the house fell silent.

"Oh, Billy," she whispered into the darkness, tearfully, "I love you."

Billy's journey home took over an hour, as he trudged from William Lane in the east of Dundee, to Lochee in the West. The night was black but the sky was full of stars and a full moon shone down on him to light his way. He was glad of the walk, as the cold night air blew the anger from his soul. He had almost come to blows with Joe Cassiday but couldn't understand why! It had felt almost as though Joe was a jealous lover instead of Nancy's father. Pictures of Nancy formed in his head and he smiled. She was a beauty alright and he wanted her badly.

His mother's voice called gently into the darkness as he entered the door of their two-roomed house in the backlands of 'Tipperary'.

"Is that you, Billy?"

"Yes, Ma," he whispered back. "I didn't mean to wake you, I'm sorry."

He heard his mother scrape a match on its box and light the small candle beside her bed. She blinked in the brightness of the illumination before sinking back onto her pillow.

"Your da's not home yet," she stated worriedly, I thought you were him."

Billy squinted at the clock on the mantelpiece. "It's past two o'clock in the morning!" he exclaimed. "When were you expecting him?"

"Around eleven, I suppose," Billy's mother replied, her eyes closed but her mind awake, "but you never know, once he gets to drinkin' and if the craic's good."

Billy frowned. "It's still mighty late for him to be out," he said, "do you want me to go look for him?"

"Oh, he'd just get angry," she said, "and anyway, you're home now, so I feel better."

"OK Ma," Billy replied, "try to get some sleep, I'll watch out till he's back."

Billy sat down in his father's chair by the dead fire and stirred the ashes. The room was cold and he pulled the collar of his jacket up round his ears. The clock ticked out the minutes, then the hours, and the grey streaks of dawn were forming in the sky when he awoke from an aching slumber.

He squinted at the clock. "Christ," he muttered, "it's gone five in the morning."

He shivered as he crossed the room to his mother's bed.

"Ma," he whispered. "Ma, wake up."

Billy's mother stirred and wakened.

"Da's not come home," he whispered, "have you any idea where he could be?"

Mrs Donnelly forced herself up on her elbows. Her face was fixed with worry.

"No, Billy," she said, "I don't." She clutched the arm of her son and pulled him towards her. "You don't think he's had an accident... do you? Or worse?"

Billy could see the panic filling her eyes as the words took shape in her heart.

"No Ma," he soothed. "C'mon, get yourself up and make some tea and I'll go lookin' for him. Somebody must know where he is." His voice sounded more confident than he felt as he tried to keep the knot of fear from tightening his muscles.

The loud banging on the door made them both jump.

Billy sat his mother down in a chair. "I'll go," he said, "sit here."

Mrs Donnelly grasped the arms of the chair as Billy went to the door.

She could hear voices and feet shuffling in the lobby. Billy's white face came round the door followed by the dark blue serge uniform of Constable O'Rourke.

"Ma," Billy said hoarsely, "it's Da… he's in jail!"

Billy's mother clutched at the shawl round her shoulders. "JAIL!" she echoed, her lips quivering with cold and fear. Constable O'Rourke removed his helmet and placed it on the kitchen table.

"I'm sorry Mrs Donnelly," he said, "to be the bearer of bad news for you, sure I know you're a good, hard-working woman…"

"What is it?" she asked. "Is he alright?"

The policeman cleared his throat.

"I'm afraid," he said formally, "Mr Donnelly was arrested at 9 p.m. last night in Murphey's Bar on a fraud charge."

"FRAUD," Billy exclaimed in disbelief. "Who the hell has he cheated for Christ's sake? He can barely read and write."

Constable O'Rourke levelled his eyes at Billy. "Language son," he said, "there is no need for blasphemy."

Billy rolled his eyes skywards. "Please, Constable O'Rourke, who's he in bother with?"

"Mr Michael Flannaghan," replied the blue-uniformed messenger smartly.

Billy's mother looked at him, shaking her head.

"Who's Michael Flannaghan?" she asked, confusion and worry uniting in harmony to knit her brows together.

Billy ran his fingers through his dark hair in amazement.

"He's the bookie… from Polepark!"

Chapter 8

"Lexie," hissed Sarah from her hiding place at the back of the close leading to Lexie's home, "over here."

Lexie squinted into the dimness of the close, inching closer till she could make out the pale face of Sarah Dawson.

"What ARE you doing, Sarah?" she asked, annoyance edging her voice as Sarah stepped forward clutching her schoolbag to her chest.

"I had to see you before we went to school," she said anxiously, undoing the leather bag and revealing her white smock liberally smeared with grass stains. "LOOK!"

Lexie pursed her lips.   Well?" she asked, not in the mood for conundrums.

Sarah took a deep breath. "Davie Robertson!"

Lexie shrugged. "What about him?"

"He was awful, Lexie," Sarah began, her eyes widening at the memory. "He chased me through the park and pulled me to the ground and…"

"And?"

Sarah hung her head. "And, he tried to KISS me!"

Lexie tried to stifle a laugh, adding to Sarah's offence. She could feel tears stinging her eyes. "And it's all your fault," she railed. "I never wanted to go to the park in the first place and if my mum sees this…" She held the garment in front of her, wishing somehow it would just disappear.

Lexie took it from her. "Leave it with me," she said, "I'll get my mother to clean it for you."

"But, what if…?"

Lexie stopped her mid-sentence. "It's alright," she said emphatically, "I'll say it was my fault. We were horsing around and you fell."

Sarah shut up.

"I'll see you at school," Lexie called over her shoulder, leaving Sarah dumbstruck as she made her way into Albert Street, "and don't worry about your smock," she added, "everything'll be alright."

It was dinner time before Sarah saw Lexie again. Despite her promise to herself never to speak to her again, she walked over to where she was holding court, surrounded by giggling girls.

Lexie saw her approaching and broke away from the crowd.

She put her arm around Sarah's shoulder. "Sorry," she said, "I didn't mean for you to get into any trouble." Sarah felt all her resolve dissipate

"It's alright," she said quietly, "I'm just not much good where boys are concerned, not like you."

Lexie smiled, remembering Robbie Robertson and his kisses. "I think I'm in love," she said softly, "with Robbie."

Sarah frowned. "How do you know?"

Lexie looked at her friend with all the experience of her 'almost fifteen' years. "I just know," she replied mysteriously. "We're meeting again next Sunday in Baxters Park and…"

Sarah jumped back. "I'm not going with you!" she exclaimed, panic raising her voice to a high pitch. She couldn't go through that ordeal again, no matter how much Lexie begged her. But Lexie didn't beg nor even ask, she just smiled enigmatically and rejoined her group of waiting admirers.

The stern look on her mother's face gave Sarah the first indication that something was wrong.

"I had a visitor to the school today," she began, her eyes fixed on those of her daughter's, "who was concerned about YOU."

A nerve in Sarah's chin quivered involuntarily.

"ME?" she enquired squeakily.

Sarah's mother clasped her hands in front of her. "Is there anything you want to tell me?" she asked.

Sarah's heart began to race. She shook her head.

"If I tell you my visitor was Lexie Melville's mother, have you still nothing to tell me?"

Sarah felt the blood drain from her face as panic gripped her heart. But she shook her head again, torn between fear and shame.

"She was returning this." Sarah's mother reached down to a loosely wrapped brown paper parcel leaning against the side of the armchair and placed it in front of Sarah.

"Now, is there anything you want to tell me?"

The tension and guilt was too much for Sarah and a huge sob erupted from somewhere deep inside of her.

"I didn't want to go," she wailed, "Lexie made me, and I'll never speak to her again."

Sarah's mother winced. So, Annie Melville had been right. Her daughter was hiding something from her AND it involved Lexie.

"Tell me what happened," she said, trying to keep her voice steady, fearful of the answer she might get.

Between sniffs, Sarah told her mother of her unhappy encounter with Davie Robertson and how Lexie had arranged it all.

"And that's everything?" Josie asked as Sarah lapsed into a miserable silence.

She nodded. "I'm sorry," she said in a small voice, "I'll never speak to Lexie Melville again."

Josie felt a wave of relief wash over her. Her daughter was growing up, there was no denying that, but for now, she was satisfied that she was still her little girl.

But, Lexie Melville, now that was a different story. She was growing up fast and couldn't wait to leave school, with its restrictions and childish rules. She'd be fifteen next birthday and was fed up with everyone telling her what to do.

"I'm leaving school and you can't stop me," she'd shouted at Annie, when her mother had tried to encourage her to stay on. "I'm going to be a weaver, like you were and like Nancy is, I don't want to stay at school like Sarah Dawson."

Annie had sighed and given in. She had inherited her Auntie Mary's fiery nature and her father's stoic determination, a combination which neither she nor Euan could control.

"I don't know what to do with her," Annie moaned to Euan on his return from duty at the police station in Bell Street. "She doesn't want to stay on at school and says she's going to work in the mills and she's up to something involving Sarah Dawson, and I just don't know what it is." She recounted the story of Sarah's smock and her meeting with Josie Dawson.

Euan sighed. "She's growing up, Annie," he said resignation in his words, "let's just hope we've brought her up with enough common sense to deal with life.

The late afternoon sun was setting as Lexie made her way to Baxters Park and her meeting with Robbie Robertson. She'd thought of nothing else for days now and everything in the park seemed to be rustling and whispering with excitement all around her. Robbie was waiting by the park gate and her heart leapt at the sight of him.

He took her hand in his and pulled her towards him. "Have you miss'd me?" he asked, crushing her fingers with his. Lexie nodded.

"I have," she said coyly, "have you missed me?"

Robbie's eyes flashed, young blood coursing through him and Lexie's smile arousing his desire for her.

"C'mon," he said urgently, "there's somethin' I want to show you."

Robbie led her to a distant corner of the park, away from the main paths and pulled her down beside him in the shade of a pink rhododendron bush.

"Look," he said, producing a tiny box from his pocket. Lexie took the box and opened it.

"It's a ring," she breathed in disbelief, gazing at the silver circle glinting in the sun, "but where did you get it?"

"Dixon's Pawn Shop," he stated proudly, "in Blackscroft. I've been savin' for ages to buy it."

Lexie's eyes widened with pride and wonder. "It's for you," Robbie said almost reverently, "so you ken how much… I love you."

Lexie thought her heart would melt. "Oh Robbie," she whispered, "do you? Do you really?"

Robbie nodded, his pale face colouring with a sudden blush of shyness which came from an unknown source awakening inside him. He took the ring from its box and pushed it onto Lexie's finger. "There," he said, "now we're engaged to be married."

Lexie gazed first at the silver ring then at the face of her first love. "Married?" she echoed, suddenly feeling very strange.

"Just as soon as you're sixteen," Robbie stated, "then we'll show them."

Lexie's grown up feelings were rapidly deserting her. She was in love, she was sure of that, but MARRIAGE!?

Chapter 9

"Will you come and cheer me on Nancy?" asked Joe, trying to keep the tension out of his voice as he polished his shoes with an energy he hadn't felt in a long time.

"Cheer you on?" queried Nancy, knowing exactly what he meant. Joe was making his first professional appearance as a singer, on stage at the Black Watch Club and she knew he wanted her there.

Joe gritted his teeth. "Aye, Nancy," he continued, "you know, at the Club this Saturday."

Nancy could feel a tingle of apprehension up her spine. "Oh, that," she said blandly, rising from the chair and heading for the door through to the back room. "Sorry, but I can't manage this Saturday."

The shoe brush hit the wooden bunker lid like a shot from a gun and Nancy stopped in her tracks.

Joe turned to face her, his mouth fixed in a grim line. "Why not?"

Nancy felt the tingle in her back turn to an ache as her body prepared for Joe's anger.

"I'm going dancing," she said, "to the Proggie with Lizzie Green." She waited, her heart pounding in her chest. "And anyway, Agnes wants to…"

Joe's hands folded into fists. "I don't want Agnes to be there," he interrupted, "I want you to be there."

The adrenalin was surging now and Nancy heard her voice shout back. "Well, I'm not going to be there," she said, "and YOU CAN'T MAKE

ME!"

Both Irish tempers held their ground and Joe backed off. He didn't want Nancy like this, he wanted her willingly and happy to be there.

"No," he said, "I can't make you, but I'm asking you. Will you come on Saturday?"

Nancy's rapid breathing slowed slightly. She wanted to see Billy Donnelly, not Joe, and Saturday was the only day of the week this was possible. She hated Joe for the feeling of guilt that his attentions brought to her soul. It wasn't her fault he was a cripple after all and she'd never asked him to put her before Agnes. Her young mind held only confusion.

"Only if Agnes comes too," she said, eventually, "and only this once."

His eyes held hers and she could see the light returning to them.

"Right you are Nancy," he said softly, "whatever you say."

Without further words, Nancy turned and disappeared through into the dimness of the back room.

She flung herself onto her bed and gazed up at the gloomy ceiling. She knew if she antagonised Joe further, there would be even more likelihood that he'd stop Billy from seeing her and she couldn't bear that. She closed her eyes and conjured up a picture of her love, which set up a longing in her heart and a heat in her body.

Agnes's voice drifted through her reverie. She was back from her cleaning job at Maryfield Hospital and Joe was telling her about Saturday.

"I'll no' let you doon," she said, elated that Joe wanted her to be there, "I'll clap louder than them all put together."

"Nancy's going too," she heard Joe say. Then silence.

Nancy was waiting for Lizzie at the mill gate the following day.

"And Joe's forcing me to go on Saturday," she regaled, "so I can't go dancing and what if Billy meets someone else and...?"

"Calm doon," instructed Lizzie, "I'll tell him what's happened. He'll understand."

She squeezed her friend's arm. "There's aye next week," Lizzie winked, "an' you ken what they say about absence makin' the heart grow fonder."

Nancy felt better. "You're right," she said, "just remember to tell him I'm sorry I couldn't be there and that I'll..."

The sound of the 'bummer' wailed its signal that the mill gate was closing and any worker who was late, or not at their task would have their wages docked, ending any further conversation for the girls.

The Black Watch Club was usually the preserve of the men only, but this was a special occasion and the committee had agreed to allow the wives of their members to attend, just this once. It was George Grant's intention that his Concert Party should tour Scotland, and the Black Watch Club was to be their dress rehearsal. If all went to plan, his band of entertainers would be on the road for three months and make him a very nice profit.

Joe was chain smoking in the tiny space he'd been allocated. The black suit and starched shirt sat well on his still-muscular frame and his hair shone with Brilliantine. He looked at himself in the piece of broken mirror, balanced on the tiny window ledge fringed with spiders' webs. He was still a good-looking man, he told himself, despite having lost one of his legs at Ypres, and although the artificial leg pained him still, at least it would allow him to stand without his crutches while he sang.

The compère's voice rang through the crowded room.

"Welcome one and all, especially the ladies," he beamed, "to the Black Watch Club."

The men leant against the mahogany bar or joined their wives with their glasses of ale in the rows of wooden chairs which had been set out for the concert.

"Order, please, one and all," he continued, raising a hand to hush the babble of voices, "for a very special evening's entertainment." The talking stopped and he cleared his throat.

"It is with great pleasure," he announced, "that we bring you this evening the very entertaining and exciting George Grant's Concert Party."

Nancy and Agnes applauded along with the rest of the crowd.

"And to begin this evening's programme, I am proud to present to you, making his first professional appearance on stage ANYWHERE, Dundee's own Irish balladeer, MR JOSEPH CASSIDAY!" His arm swept behind him and the curtains on the small stage parted.

Joe's eyes scanned the audience for Nancy, as a wave of warm applause greeted him.

"She's here," he breathed to himself, spotting her in the third row with Agnes, and he would sing tonight, just for her.

The piano and accordion began to play. "If I were a blackbird," sang Joe, "I'd whistle and sing, and follow the ship that my true love sails in…" His voice rang clear and strong. "I'll take you home again, Kathleen, across the ocean wild and wide, to where the hills are evergreen, when first you were my blushing bride…" Barmen stopped pouring out ale, men sipped their whiskey with misty eyes, and Nancy sat transfixed at the beauty of the sound.

She'd heard Joe sing around the house, now and then, but nothing like this.

"Oh, Agnes," she whispered.

"Ssssshhhhh," a voice behind her cautioned.

Joe finished with 'When You Were Sweet Sixteen', which he sang directly to Nancy.

As the last notes of the song died, the room erupted in applause.

"Bravo," the men called. "More, more."

The compère returned to the stage, wiping tears from his eyes.

"Ladies and gentlemen," he said gruffly, "I'm sure Mr Cassiday will return later in the evening to sing for us once more, but for now, waiting in the wings is our next turn, the one and only DIXIE GRIFFIN!" He began clapping his hands and the audience followed as Dixie made his entrance.

"Follow THAT!" he exclaimed, smiling widely, before launching into his patter.

Joe gulped down a glass of ale and wiped the sweat from his brow. He was a triumph and Nancy had been there to see it. For now, he was satisfied.

Chapter 10

There was an uncomfortable silence while Constable O'Rourke let the news of Billy's father's arrest sink in.

"What happens now?" Billy asked quietly, gathering his mother into his arms. "I mean, can we see him? See he's alright?"

The policeman cleared his throat. "He's being held in the cells at Bell Street till the court sits on Monday. They'll decide then what's to be done." He replaced his helmet and indicated to Billy to follow him to the door, eyeing with concern the shocked figure of Billy's mother.

"You're quite welcome to see him, Billy," he said with a fatherly concern. He'd known the Donnelly family since Billy was a lad and he also knew of Mr Donnelly's fondness for the 'nags'. "But the jail isn't any place for your mother to see, if you know what I mean."

Billy nodded. He didn't know what he meant, but could imagine and a huge rush of compassion filled him for his father's plight.

Constable O'Rourke pressed Billy's shoulder with his huge hand.

"Come down around eight o'clock," he said kindly, "and look after your mammy, Billy, she's had a bit of a shock."

Billy's mother was on her knees shovelling grey ashes from the grate into a galvanised bucket.

"I'll do that Ma," he said, kneeling beside her and trying to remove the shovel from her trembling fingers. But she held on to it.

"No Billy," she said, her voice trembling with cold and apprehension, "I

44

need to be busy."

Billy squeezed her frail body in understanding. "Constable O'Rourke says I can see Da at eight o'clock. Will you be alright till I get back?"

Billy's mother stopped raking the ashes. "You're not going without me," she said, anxiously. "Your Da may not be perfect, but he's not a bad man, Billy, and…" Her resolve faded as the fear won. "I just need to see him," she ended quietly. "He'd expect it."

"I'll make us some tea," Billy said gently, "then we'll go and see Da… together."

The long walk down Lochee Road to Bell Street helped calm Billy's mind. He always found walking helped, sometimes, when he'd had enough of the smoke and noise and smell of jute he'd take off into the rolling hills of Strathmartine, with just a bottle of water and a handful of raisins from his mother's kitchen cupboard. They passed Dudhope Park and Billy could see the spires of the infirmary reaching up to the Law Hill behind them. "Nearly there," he said, "are you alright?"

Billy's mother nodded.

The iron gates of the jail in Bell Street were open and lead into a grey cobbled courtyard flanked on two sides by the cells where the prisoners were kept. Tiny grated windows ranged along the walls, allowing light to filter in along with the cold wind that swirled around the courtyard.

Mrs Donnelly clutched her son's hand.

"We're here to see William Donnelly," Billy said to the policeman standing guard at a stout wooden door, studded with iron bolts and hinges. "Can we see him?"

"Relation are you?" asked the emotionless voice.

"Son," replied Billy, "and this is me mother, I mean, Mrs Donnelly."

The policeman unhooked a huge bunch of keys from a metal ring which hung from his belt and opened the creaking door.

"Through there," he nodded, "ask for the duty sergeant."

A smell like boiled cabbage and fish mixed with despair wafted over them as the door clanged behind them.

Euan MacPherson looked up from behind his desk. He hated when prisoner's wives came to visit, they were always so pitiful, and the one before him was no exception.

"Are you the duty sergeant?" asked Billy nervously.

Euan nodded and looked at Billy's mother, small and frail, worn down by hard work and poverty and now, this.

"Can we see William Donnelly, please?"

Euan's eyes narrowed in concern. "Are you his son?" Euan asked.

"It might be best if your mother waits here," he said kindly, "just for a minute. Give Mr Donnelly a chance to tidy himself for his visitors."

Billy guided his mother to a wooden chair against the wall of the duty room.

"I'll be back in a minute," he whispered, fear suddenly taking root in his stomach, "I'll tell Da you're here."

Euan unhooked the large iron key from its place on the wall beside the door leading to the cells. "This way, son," he said, "I'm afraid Mr Donnelly's taking his incarceration quite badly and it might be best if Mrs Donnelly didn't see him right now."

Billy felt his heart begin to pound in his chest as he followed the sergeant down the stone stairs and into the dimness of the corridor leading to the cells. All his senses were alert, his ears heard the scrape of every rat in the pipes and the moan of each inmate, his eyes focused like a cat in the dark, widening to see the rivets in each cell door and his tongue tasted the misery and hopelessness of this dark place.

His legs felt like cold lead as they carried him into the depth of the jail.

Euan MacPherson stopped and slid the cover from the viewing hole in the door of the end cell. "Visitor for you," he called through the metal. "Stand by your bed."

The heavy door swung open and Billy stepped inside.

"Bang on the door if you want to leave," Euan said, "otherwise, you've got fifteen minutes."

"Are you alright, Da?" Billy asked into the dimness and cold, painfully aware that his father was not. Somehow, his father had become an old man in that one weekend. His face sagged beneath tufts of grey hair and his shoulders drooped under the folds of the collarless shirt which covered him. His hands clutched his trousers at the waist and his bare feet were poked into laceless shoes.

"Ma's waiting," Billy continued, feeling inadequate and helpless, "she's worried about you."

His father slumped onto the iron frame of the tiny cot. "I don't want her to see me," he said, "not like this." His eyes, pale and watery and rimmed red with lack of sleep turned to his son. "You shouldn't have brought her."

"I tried to stop her coming," Billy said, "but she'd have none of it."

His father didn't answer.

"Have they given you anythin' to eat?" he asked, changing the subject away from his mother.

"The Salvation Army came in with tea and bread a while ago," Mr Donnelly whispered, his rough hands covering his face.

Billy spoke again. "What've you done Da?"

He could hear his father's breathing turn into sobs. He wished he could reach out to him, let him know he was there for him, no matter what he'd done, but he couldn't.

Instead he stood gazing at his shoes till his father regained control.

"I'm a thief, son," his father said in a thick voice.

Billy winced. "You've never stolen anything in your life, Da," he began, feeling his father's pain. "I don't believe it. There must be a mistake."

Mr Donnelly shook his head and raised his eyes to meet those of his son.

"I thought I was being clever, Billy," he whispered, "thought I'd found a way of making easy money by cheating the bookie and now, look at me..."

He turned his head away, unable to bear the shame he'd brought to his family. The clank of the key in the cell door brought the misery to an end.

"You'll have to go now, lad," Euan MacPherson said to Billy, "your mother's getting anxious."

Billy nodded. "I'll come back tomorrow morning, Da," he said through the lump in his throat.

The sergeant guided Billy back to where his mother waited.

"Is he alright, Billy," she asked anxiously, "is your Da alright?"

Billy put his arm around her shoulders. "He's fine Ma," he said softly, "just wants to be alone just now, says he'll see you when he comes home."

Billy's mother's eyes widened in pain. "You're hiding something from me," she said, gripping Billy's coat sleeves.

Sergeant MacPherson came to Billy's rescue.

"Your husband's fine, Mrs Donnelly," he said evenly, "we'll look after him for you."

"The sergeant's right," Billy said, "Da's fine. He just wants you to go home and not worry."

By the time Billy and his mother had walked slowly back to their room and kitchen in 'Tipperary' the whole of Lochee was abuzz with talk about Billy's father. Crones were gathered in clutches at close ends and shop doorways and Billy's father's peers were muttering in dark corners about how Michael Flannaghan, the bookie from Polepark, would get no more business from them.

"I need to know what happened," Billy whispered to his mother, sitting her down with a cup of tea back in the kitchen of their home. He pulled on his jacket again. "I'll be back soon," he said, "try to get some rest."

Billy ran down the stairs two at a time and headed for Polepark.

One of Michael Flannaghan's 'runners' was plying his trade at the gates of the Coffin Mill, where a scattering of men were huddled around him placing their bets.

"I'm looking for Mr Flannaghan," Billy asked, over the heads of the punters.

The 'runner' squinted around the shoulders of his customers.

"Who's lookin' for'um?" squeaked Moosey Broon, stuffing betting slips into his trouser pocket.

"Billy Donnelly."

The 'runner' paled. "If you're for causin' trouble…" he began, "dinna start wi' me."

The group of men were interested now. "I don't want trouble," Billy continued quietly, "just need to speak to Mr Flannaghan."

Moosey Broon's eyes shifted uneasily from Billy to a close entrance behind him on Polepark Road.

"You'll find'um over there," he said, "twa stairs up on the right."

"Thanks," Billy nodded.

The wooden door was opened by the burly frame of Michael Flannaghan himself.

"Well?" he said, eyeing Billy suspiciously before deciding he posed no threat.

"I've come to ask about my father, Mr Flannaghan," Billy said politely.

Michael's eyes narrowed. "And who might he be?"

"William Donnelly."

Billy just managed to get his foot in the door as Michael Flannaghan tried to slam it shut.

"Yir father's a thief," the bookie spat, "that's all you need to know. And I hope he rots in jail."

Billy felt cold anger well inside of him.

"And you'd be advised to bugger off," he continued menacingly, "before I have you lifted an' all,"

A rough hand pushed Billy backwards and the door slammed shut. Billy's heart was thudding and hot tears forced themselves from under his eyelids. He sat down heavily on the stone step at the top of the stair and gave in to the helplessness that enveloped him.

Chapter 11

Robbie gazed into Lexie's eyes.

"Well," he breathed, placing the silver ring on the third finger of her left hand, "will you?"

Lexie twisted the ring round her finger. The girls at school would be so jealous, especially Sarah. Imagine, her, Lexie Melville, engaged to be married.

"I think so," she said, coyly, before adding, "YES, Robbie, I WILL."

Robbie pulled her into his arms and squeezed her so tightly to his chest she thought she would suffocate.

"You'll no' regret it, Lexie," he vowed earnestly. "I'll work hard to give you everythin' you could ever want."

"And do you love me, Robbie?" Lexie murmured again, "I mean, reeeaaallly."

Robbie Robertson had never loved anyone so much in his life.

"Of coorse, Lexie," he replied, "an' when you're sixteen, I'll show you how much."

For all her worldliness, Lexie wasn't sure what exactly Robbie would do to show her 'how much', but for now, the thrill of being special filled her young heart to the exclusion of all else.

The young lovers strolled back through the park hand in hand, the whole world seeming to be there just for them.

"I'll meet you at the park gate the morn, when I've finished at Harry Duncan's," Robbie said proudly, "an' will you never take my ring off?" he added urgently, keenly aware that they must part for at least twenty-four hours.

Lexie's eyes sparkled their answer. "Never," she said solemnly, "never till the day I die."

"Is that you Lexie?" Annie called out at the sound of the front door opening and closing.

"It's me," Lexie answered, quickly removing the silver ring from her finger and slipping it into her pocket.

"Bring through the milk from the kitchen," her mother ordered her, "and come and get some tea."

For once, Lexie dutifully obeyed.

"Where have you been?" her mother asked. "It's getting dark out."

"Oh, just over at Sarah's," Lexie lied, "writing my composition for school tomorrow."

Annie eyed her daughter. "Are you feeling alright?" she asked, placing a cool hand on her daughter's brow. "You seem flushed."

Lexie flushed further. "Of course," she said quickly, "I've just been running to get home, that's all."

Her mother seemed satisfied.

"Here," Annie said, handing Lexie a steaming cup, "have some tea. That'll cool you down, then you can help me make supper. Your dad'll be home soon."

If Euan noticed anything different about his stepdaughter, he didn't say and the evening meal was eaten in the usual silence. Lexie made her excuses to leave the table as soon as the plates were cleared and even volunteered to wash the dishes.

Annie eyed her daughter quizzically. "Thanks, Lexie," she said, "there's a good girl that you are."

Lexie made her way out of the house and up to the school gate the following day. As she turned into the playground she slipped it back on her finger.

Jean Ogilvie was the first to notice it, as Lexie waved her hand in front of her face at every opportunity.

"Where'd you get tha'?" she asked, pointing to the silver circle.

"From my boyfriend," Lexie advised her airily.

Jean's eyes widened. "An' how come you're wearin' it on THAT finger?"

"Because," Lexie told her, affecting what she thought was an air of sophistication, "I'm engaged… to be married."

Jean Ogilvie shrieked loudly, attracting the attention of a clutch of girls waiting for the teacher's whistle to signal they should form their lines for filing into the school.

"Quick," she called out, frantically signalling anyone within hailing distance, "look what Lexie's Melville's got!"

Sarah Dawson followed the others, wondering what Lexie had got up to now.

She pushed her way through the huddle to Lexie's side.

"Robbie Robertson asked me to marry him yesterday," her friend was announcing, waving her hand in front of her admiring peers and more pointedly in front of Sarah.

"Some of us know how to handle boys," she mocked, laughing, "and some of us don't."

Sarah's face burned at the memory of Robbie's brother and her struggle with his unwanted attention.

"We're to be married, when I'm sixteen," Lexie continued, "and you're all invited."

The sound of the teacher's whistle put a stop to any further news, as the girls scurried giggling to their lines.

"You're not really going to marry Robbie Robertson, are you?" Sarah asked, amazed at her friend's news and just a bit jealous too. Lexie seemed so far ahead of her when it came to boys and she felt clumsy and pathetic.

"Of course," Lexie replied, enjoying the limelight. "And if you're not careful," she dropped her voice to a conspiratorial whisper, "you'll die an auld maid in a garrett."

Sarah gulped. This was the worst possible fate she could imagine. She'd seen the spinster teachers at the school, tight lipped and grey, and she didn't want to be like them.

"No I won't," she retorted defensively, "I'm going to university first, that's all."

Lexie sniffed. "To be a teacher, no doubt."

Hot tears of defeat stung Sarah's eyes but she turned and walked away quickly before Lexie could see them.

"I was only joking," she called after the disappearing back of her friend, but Sarah had closed her ears and her heart.

"I won't be an old maid," she told herself firmly, "no matter what Lexie said."

The day dragged till, at last, the school bell rang for the last time and Lexie and her crowd were disgorged from the classroom back into the reality of the streets of Dundee. Jean Ogilvie led the procession of curious girls from the school gate, down Forfar Road and into Stobswell, giggling all the while and each straining to catch a glimpse of the ring. Much to Lexie's chagrin, the obvious exception was Sarah, who had slipped quickly past the throng and, head down, had gone home alone.

Lexie hadn't meant to hurt her friend's feelings and she would tell her she was sorry later, but for now, she basked in the attention of the rest of the girls.

"And I'm seeing Robbie tonight," she told the enthralled audience, "and we're going to plan our future… together."

The gaggle reached the entrance to the close leading to Lexie's home, which ended any further speculation, as Lexie disappeared into its dark mouth, slipping off the ring as she did so. She was sure she was in love with Robbie Robertson, but the prospect of telling her mother of her engagement filled her with shivers of fear.

Lexie quickly ate the sandwiches and scones her mother had laid out for her.

"Is it alright if I go to Sarah's again?" she called over her shoulder to Annie, as she gulped down the last of her cup of tea, before pushing the chair away from the table. "We've more homework to do and the exams are at the end of this month…"

"Yes, yes," her mother replied absently, barely glancing up as she scrubbed her son's knees with carbolic soap and a nail brush.

"How someone so small can attract so much dirt," she admonished Ian MacPherson, "I just don't know."

Lexie heard her brother's squeals as the nail brush scraped across his skin, but was out of the door before her mother could change her mind.

Robbie was waiting at the park gate. His unruly hair had been parted at the side and flattened down with water and his broad shoulders took up more room than his jacket would permit, leaving his arms dangling out of the sleeve ends.

"Lexie," he breathed, as she neared him, "you're here."

He clasped her hands in his.

"Are you still gonna marry me?" he asked anxiously, as through the last twenty-four hours had somehow managed to change her mind.

Lexie nodded.

"Good," he said, satisfied, "an' are you still wearin' it then?"

He lifted Lexie's left hand and smiled as the little silver band glowed on her finger.

"What time've you to be home?"

"About eight o'clock," Lexie said, "I'm supposed to be at Sarah's, doing homework."

"We've got two hours then," he said huskily, glancing at the clock tower of Morgan School. "Time enough."

Robbie led her into the park, clutching her hand in his and breathing heavily as they climbed the slope towards the spot where he'd given her the ring.

They both flopped down onto the grass, gazing at the trees swaying gently above them, and conscious of the warmth of their bodies against the cold ground. Robbie pulled Lexie towards him.

"Now we're engaged to be married," he whispered, "it's alright if we go... further."

"Where to?" Lexie asked innocently.

"You ken where," Robbie replied hotly, pulling her tighter. "Further than kissin'."

Lexie felt her body tense in panic as the realisation of Robbie's intention came home to her.

"But, I've never done anything like THAT," she said, fear taking hold as she tried to sit upright and failed.

"You dinna have to do anythin'," Robbie urged, easily pinning her arms above her head, "just dinna struggle."

She could hear a dog barking in the distance. "Someone's coming," she squeaked, her voice faint with terror. "STOP, Robbie, please, we'll get into trouble."

But Robbie wasn't for stopping.

Chapter 12

For two weeks now, the town had been buzzing with talk of the forthcoming trial of Billy's father. Finally, the day of judgement arrived. Billy sat anxiously with his mother in the gallery of the courtroom surrounded by an assorted crowd of Lochee millworkers and Dundee worthies, many of whom were familiar to him and some who were not.

'Your dad's a fine man, Billy," whispered Ernie Dobbie, a neighbour from 'Tipperary'. "The judge'll see tha'." Billy nodded as Ernie squeezed his arm in assurance. "We'll all be keepin' our fing'rs crossed." He indicated the row of concerned faces behind them. "Me and the boys'll be sortin' out Mik Flannaghan if your dad's found guilty." He tapped the side of his nose. "Ken what I mean?"

Billy flinched, his father was in enough trouble as it was without inciting a riot.

The sound of the judge's gavel pounding the desk in front of him ended any further conversation and the Clerk of the Court announced the next case.

"William Donnelly," he intoned. There was a pause while Billy's father was brought from the cells and mounted the steps into the courtroom. Billy leaned forward to see him better and shuddered at the whiteness of his face and the stoop of his shoulders.

He clasped his mother's hand in his. "It'll all be over soon," he whispered, "and, God willing, he'll be home."

The charge was read out to its listening audience. "William Donnelly, you are charged that on the day of Saturday 20th March 1928 you presented a betting slip to Michael Flannaghan, of 25 Polepark Dundee, knowing that it had been altered to show a winning line, after the horse race had been run and in so doing, caused Mr Flannaghan to hand over to you £5. 2/6d." The clerk raised his head. "How do you plead?"

Mr Donnelly's voice was barely audible. "Not guilty."

A murmur of approval rippled round the court.

"Silence," instructed the procurator, banging his gavel once more, onto its wooden base.

"Mr O'Hara." He eyed the diminutive solicitor on the front bench. "You may proceed."

"I would like to call Michael Flannaghan to the witness box," he said, rummaging through a pile of papers in front of him.

The call went out and Michael Flannaghan was ushered into the witness box and sworn in. George O'Hara peered at him over his half-moon glasses.

"What is your profession, Mr Flannaghan," he asked quietly.

The bookmaker cleared his throat. "Accountant," he stated, loudly. Muffled laughter erupted from the gallery.

"And by *accountant*," continued O'Hara, "do you mean you, perhaps, handle people's finances for them?"

Mik Flannaghan's face reddened. "You could say that."

Billy and his mother leaned further forward, not wanting to miss a word of the cross-examination.

"And would it be true to say, that sometimes, just sometimes, you use your clients' money for *investment purposes?*"

Mik shifted uncomfortably in the witness box. "Do I have tae answer that, Your Honour?" he asked. "After all, it's me that's been robbed."

"Answer the question," the procurator ordered curtly.

"Sometimes," the bookie murmured.

"And would it also be true to say…" George O'Hara's eyes ranged over the courtroom… "that this sometimes, just sometimes, would result in an investment in… HORSEFLESH?"

A roar of approval rang through the room.

The procurator hammered his gavel for silence. "Another interruption like that," he shouted, "and I'll clear this court."

The reporter from the Dundee Courier scribbled furiously, sensing a human interest story unfolding in front of him. His editor would love it; stories like this always sold papers.

"Mr Flannaghan," O'Hara said quietly, "and how did you *invest* Mr Donnelly's money on the day in question.

Mik Flannaghan's face was contorting in anger. "Everybody kens how it was INVESTED," he shouted. "The cheatin' wee runt."

"Mr Flannaghan," interrupted the procurator, his voice rising in agitation at the disruption in his courtroom, "answer the question."

"I bet it on a horse!" Mik replied through clenched teeth.

George O'Hara shook his head and removed his glasses.

"Mr Flannaghan," he began sweetly, "are you not aware that in this country, betting on the horses is… ILLEGAL?"

The air filled with loud laughter and Billy held his mother's hand tightly.

"Your Honour," continued the solicitor, removing his glasses and nodding his head towards Billy's father. "I would suggest that in this case, there is no case to answer."

The Judge's eyes went from Mik Flannaghan to Billy's father and back to George O'Hara.

"I think, Mr O'Hara," the procurator nodded sagely, the beginnings of a smile forming on his lips, that in this case, you might be quite right. His gavel came down with a resounding smack. "The verdict is," he intoned loudly, "that William Donnelly be ADMONISHED and leave this court without a stain to his character."

Billy leapt to his feet amid the cheering crowd as the reporter ran from the courtroom to type up his story for the next day's edition of the Dundee Courier.

"C'mon, Ma," he whispered, steering her through the line of back-slapping supporters, "let's get him home."

They hurried out of the courtroom and round to the jail where Euan MacPherson was completing the paperwork on Billy's father.

"You're a lucky man, Mr Donnelly," he said wisely, "let this be a lesson to you and, I hope, I never see you in here again."

William Donnelly hung his head. "You won't, Sergeant," he said shamefully, "you can be sure of that."

"I think that's maybe your good lady and your son coming for you," Euan added, indicating the approaching figures of Mrs Donnelly and Billy.

"You've a fine son there, make sure you thank him for standing by you."

Mr Donnelly's chin quivered as he fought to control his emotions. "I will," he said hoarsely as Billy's arm wrapped itself round his shoulders.

"Can we go home now?" Mrs Donnelly asked Euan anxiously.

Euan nodded. "And I'm sure that'll be the end of it," he whispered gently.

The small family nodded in unison and, together, left the duty room to face the future.

"What was all that about Sergeant?" asked Jimmy Spiers, Euan's duty constable,

Euan sighed. "It was about justice, Jimmy," he replied, "something the law sometimes doesn't know much about."

Jimmy pursed his slips and shrugged. "Would you like a cup o' tea, Sergeant?" he asked blandly. Euan smiled. "That would be very nice Constable Spiers and I'll have two sugars and maybe even a garibaldi biscuit."

The following morning the Dundee Courier made the most of the story, and Joe Cassiday read the paper with unconcealed glee.

"Didn't I tell you he was a layabout?" he announced to Nancy, waving the paper in front of her.

Nancy flinched as she read the story.

"…William Donnelly was today admonished at the Dundee Courthouse on a charge of fraud, due to the technicality that the money in question was used for illegal purposes by Mr Michael Flannaghan of Polepark, Dundee…"

"Like father like son, I always say," added Joe knowingly, "just as well old Joe's a better judge of character than most, eh Nancy?"

Nancy bit her lip. *So, that was why Billy hadn't been at the dancing for the past two weeks. Poor Billy, it must have been awful for him.*

Her eyes levelled with Joe's. "So, you'll have no need to worry now, will you?" Nancy told him evenly, "and you can go on the tour with the Concert Party with a clear mind."

Agnes watched the sparring match and Nancy was winning. Ever since Joe's success at the Black Watch Club, he'd been going from strength to strength on stage and was determined to be part of George Grant's Scottish Tour. His only fear had been leaving Nancy behind for three months when the tour began on 1st of April, but now the Donnelly family had been shamed he felt easier. Surely Nancy would have the sense to stay away from Billy Donnelly and his feckless father.

Joe's fingers gripped Nancy's arms. "Promise me," he said harshly, his eyes narrowing as they sought reassurance from his stepdaughter, "that while I'm gone, you won't let Donnelly near you?"

Nancy's jaw tightened. "His name's Billy."

"PROMISE ME!" Joe's fingers tightened further.

"STOP IT JOE!" Agnes shouted nervously, coming between them and trying to prise his fingers open. "I'll make sure she doesn't see him. TRUST ME."

There was a silence as Joe took in his wife's words and he slackened his grip.

"I'll find out," he said savagely, "if you do."

Nancy rubbed her arms. "Thanks Agnes," she whispered, as Joe sat down slowly in a chair, his mind agitated and afraid. He couldn't bear it if Nancy lay with another man. He'd known that for a long time now. If Billy Donnelly touched her while he was away, he'd have to kill him. In his mind, there was no other way.

Chapter 13

"Is everything alright, Lexie?"

Annie eyed her daughter with concern. For days now she hadn't seemed herself.

Lexie nodded silently.

"You're not coming down with anything are you?"

"I'm fine," Lexie snapped back, "just leave me alone."

Annie's eyebrows shot up at the angry reply.

"Hey, hey," she said, part soothingly and part in admonishment, "there is something wrong…what is it?"

Lexie could feel tears welling in her eyes and her chin began to quiver uncontrollably.

"I'm fed up of that silly school," she began shakily, "I keep telling you I want to leave."

Annie crossed to where her daughter was sitting, her head drooped in dejection.

"Why, Lexie," she began, worried now for her daughter, "what's brought this on again?"

Lexie clutched her arms around her stomach and remembered Robbie's harsh penetration of her. She had bled that night and her legs had hurt.

"Nothing," she murmured. "I just want to leave that's all, and go to work."

Annie sighed and put her arm around her daughter's shoulders.

"I know you're more grown up than the rest of the girls," she said, "but it won't be long now, it'll be summer before you know it…"

"I don't want to wait till then," Lexie interrupted, "I want to leave NOW."

Sensing one of Lexie's determined moods, Annie gave up.

"I'll speak to your father when he comes in," she said, her voice heavy with resignation, "he'll know what's best."

Lexie sniffed.

She had hated what Robbie had done to her and didn't feel nearly as grown up as everyone thought she was, especially Robbie. The thought of him near her again filled her with dread and the shame she felt threatened to overwhelm her usually confident disposition. In her young mind, she believed more than ever that, somehow, if she was working, no one would then be able to tell her what to do, not her mother nor Euan nor ROBBIE.

Annie tweaked the curtains for the hundredth time and peered out into the gloom of the wet afternoon. "C'mon Euan," she muttered, "don't be late home today, not today."

Her mind was more agitated than she cared to admit by her daughter's behaviour. Lexie was always on her 'high horse' about something but this felt different. Annie had picked up on an emotion not usually associated with her daughter. FEAR.

She heard the even footsteps of Euan climbing the stairs to the front door and ran to open it.

"Euan," she hissed, "at last. Where have you been?"

Euan removed his helmet and looked quizzically at Annie.

"Working, Annie," he replied patiently, "as usual."

Annie hurried him into the kitchen and closed the door behind her.

"I'm worried," she began, bustling about the small room. "You've got to do something, talk some sense into her."

"Her?"

Annie flopped onto the wooden chair and leant her arms earnestly on the table.

"Lexie," Annie breathed, "she's threatening to leave school again."

Euan smiled. "Annie, lass, Lexie threatens to do something outrageous every other day, as well you know."

Annie held up her hand. "This time it's different," she said, "I don't know what's wrong with her, but this time… it's different."

Euan sighed. How many times had he heard that one?

"Alright, Annie, calm down, I'll have a word with her."

Annie relaxed. She loved her daughter dearly, but as each year had passed, she became more aware of the power of her personality and it overwhelmed her, just like her sister Mary's had done when they were young and living on the farm in Ireland.

"She's in her room," Annie said, nodding towards the door of the kitchen.

"Now?" asked Euan.

Annie nodded. "Please."

Euan knocked softly on the door of Lexie's room. There was no response. Turning the handle slowly, he pushed the door open.

Lexie lay on her bed, staring at the ceiling.

"Didn't you hear me knocking?" Euan asked quietly.

"No," Lexie replied, her gaze fixed on the fringe trimming the shade of the electric light in the centre of the ceiling.

Euan closed the door behind him and pulled up the basket chair from beside the small dressing table under the window.

"Mind if I sit for a while?" he asked, trying to gauge the mood of his stepdaughter.

Annie was right, he thought, *something is very wrong.*

Lexie shrugged and swung her legs over the edge of the bed and onto the floor.

"Please yourself," she said cheekily, "I'm going out."

"Sit down, Lexie," Euan ordered, his voice taking on the authority he normally reserved for his constables.

Lexie's eyes glittered with defiance, but she did as she was told.

"Now," continued Euan, "are you going to tell me what's wrong?"

Lexie sighed and fought to control the blobs of wetness which were rapidly forming on the lower lids of her young eyes.

"I suppose Mum's sent you up," she said, more as a statement than a question.

"She's worried, Lexie," Euan said gently, "and so am I."

Lexie clasped her hands together tightly on her lap. She wished she was dead.

"I just want to leave school, that's all," she said, bowing her head to conceal the shame she felt, "go to work in the mills, like Nancy."

Euan nodded silently. "Very commendable," he said, "but not very wise."

Lexie began twisting the edge of her cardigan and poking her fingers through the buttonholes. How she wished she'd never met Robbie Robertson.

"Don't you think there'll be plenty of time to work when the school term ends in August?" Euan continued. "It's only a few months away."

Euan's understanding voice was more than Lexie could bear and she burst into a gush of guilty tears.

"Lexie, Lexie," Euan said, more worried than ever, "tell me what it is, please?"

For a long time, his stepdaughter sobbed in his arms, till finally, all cried out, she sat up and took a deep breath.

"It's Robbie Robertson," she began, her composure returning. "We're ENGAGED to be married."

"MARRIED!" echoed Euan. Many thoughts had gone through his mind as Lexie had wept, but this definitely hadn't been one of them. "But, you're just a child," he said, stunned at the announcement, "and who's Robbie Robertson?"

Lexie blinked through red-rimmed eyes. "He's the butcher's lad at Harry Duncan's in King Street."

Euan winced at the child-like tone of her answer. "Young love, eh?" he replied, trying to gain his own composure and wishing Annie would come through, this was more her department than his.

"I think your mother might have a thing or two to say about this," he said lamely, "and I think maybe I should be having a word with Mr Robertson!"

Lexie bit her lip. "I don't want to get married," she said earnestly, "it's just that…"

Euan took her hands. "What?" he asked, suddenly aware of the implications of 'young love and a healthy butcher's lad'.

"It's just that… I don't know how to tell him I've changed my mind," Lexie stammered, handing Euan the silver ring and ducking out of admitting the real reason for her tears.

Euan shook his head. She was a lovely girl, just blossoming into womanhood and ripe for the picking. He should have made more of an attempt to control her, but it had never seemed quite right, her being his stepdaughter and all.

"Is that all there is?" Euan asked, turning the ring over and over and watching her eyes for any sign of deceit, but she kept her head lowered.

"Yes," she said, softly.

"And will you give him back 'that'," she added, her eyes indicating the ring, "and tell him to go away… please?"

Euan sighed, and thanked God the situation was back in control.

"Puppy love," he told Annie, "that's gone a bit too far, that's all. I'll drop in at Harry Duncan's on the way to the station tomorrow and have a word with the lad."

"Are you sure that's all, Euan?" Annie pressed, "I mean…"

Euan shrugged. "I think so, Annie," he said, "let's just trust her for now, eh?"

Annie nodded. But she remembered her own youth and Billy Dawson and how it had felt to be in love with him.

Lexie came into the front room. "I'm sorry, Mammy," she said, her youthfulness crying out to be understood. Annie opened her arms.

"It's alright, Lexie," she said, gathering her up, "Euan'll have a word with Robbie tomorrow and we'll speak of it no more."

Lexie nodded into Annie's breasts.

"And let's have no more talk of leaving school," she said, matter-of-fact now, glad the situation was out in the open. "Go and fetch your brother now," she continued, "tea's nearly ready and I bet you're starving."

Lexie nodded, determined to do everything she was told from now on to wipe out the stain of guilt that filled her mind. "Thanks Mammy," she said almost shyly, kissing Annie's cheek. "I love you."

Annie flustered at the unaccustomed show of affection from her daughter.

"G'way with you," she smiled, glancing at Euan in embarrassment.

"Will you make sure you see that young lad tomorrow?" she whispered as Lexie disappeared into the lobby.

"Yes, yes," nodded Euan, "he'll be told to stay away from Lexie from now on if he knows what's good for him."

But Robbie Robertson had different ideas.

Chapter 14

Joe had been on tour barely a week when Billy Donnelly called on Nancy.

Agnes had opened the door to the tall, rangy frame of Billy and flinched at the sight of his handsome face.

"Is Nancy in?" he asked politely. "Can you tell her Billy wants to speak with her? Billy Donnelly."

Agnes drew back into the dimness of the lobby.

"Nancy," she called over her shoulder, "somebody to see you."

Nancy's face appeared behind Agnes.

"Billy!" she exclaimed in a mixture of shock and delight, "why, I..."

"Sorry to just arrive like this, but I couldn't think of any other way to see you."

His eyes sought hers for encouragement to continue. "Is it alright?"

Nancy's eyes drifted from Billy to Agnes. "Well?" she said. "IS it alright?"

Nancy threw Agnes a pleading glance. *She wouldn't tell Joe, would she?*

"Of course it is, Billy," she managed to say, feigning a lightness she didn't feel. "I'll just get my coat and you can take me for a walk."

Billy grinned. "I'll wait at the end of the close," he said, "just in case your dad's around."

Agnes closed the door and faced Nancy. "An' he can thank his lucky stars Joe's no' around," she said through tight lips, "at least no' this time."

Nancy swung her coat over her shoulders.

"Let me past," she ordered defiantly. "I don't care what you say or what Joe says for that matter, I'm going to see Billy and no one's going to stop me."

For a moment the two women sized one another up before Agnes moved aside to let Nancy pass.

"You'll live to regret this," she hissed as Nancy swept out. "If Joe ever finds out, you know what he'll do."

Nancy felt her blood run cold. "He'll only find out if you tell him," she retorted hoarsely, "and if you do that, you'll have lost him forever."

It was an impasse and Agnes knew it.

"Don't wait up for me," Nancy added, confident that she'd had the last word, "I'll be back late."

Billy grasped her hands and pulled her to him.

"Nancy, Nancy," he whispered, "are you alright?"

Nancy nodded and blushed. "I am now," she said, "now that you've come for me."

He linked her arm through his. "Let's walk to the Stannergate, get away from the smell of jute for a while."

Nancy nodded happily. "Anything you say, Billy," she whispered.

They took the road down St Rouques Lane past Baxters Lower Mill and across Blackscroft into Peep-O-Day Lane leading down to the River Tay. The cobbles rang beneath their feet as the sounds of the docks grew louder. Winches and cranes creaked and strained as they bore the weight of the bales of jute being unloaded onto the quays, where brawny dockers relentlessly barrowed them into the sheds on the wharf front.

Billy called out to one of them as they passed. "Hi Davie!" he shouted, "don't you be working too hard now, will you?"

A huge barrel of a man waved back. "Is it yourself Billy Donnelly?" he grinned. "And with a bonnie lassie as well"

Nancy beamed and held tighter to Billy's arm. They followed the road past the Caledon Shipyard and alongside the river to the Stannergate.

"C'mon," urged Billy, "let's dip our toes in the Tay."

"But it'll be freezing," Nancy squealed.

Billy wrapped his arms around her. "No it won't," he smiled, "I'll keep you warm."

Like five-year-olds they scrambled over the rocks and shingle down to the water's edge.

"Here," Billy said, helping Nancy to balance on a black rock, "slip your shoes and stockings off and we'll wash the cares of the world away in the Tay."

Giggling, Nancy did as she was told while Billy rolled his trouser legs up to his knees.

"There," he said grinning widely, "ready when you are."

He lifted Nancy down from the rock and together they ran the short distance to the foaming water.

"Billy, it's FREEZING!" Nancy shouted, lifting her skirt clear of the water as it lapped around her ankles. "We must be MAD!"

"Mad about you," Billy said, suddenly serious as he held her tightly around her waist.

"Oh, Billy," Nancy whispered, longing to return his affection honestly and openly, "but what about Joe… I mean, my father?"

"What about him?" Billy replied, leading her back to the rock. "Surely he wants his daughter to be happy?"

Not waiting for an answer, he bent down and rubbed Nancy's frozen feet with his hands till they dried and a surge of warmth flooded back into them. "Here," he said gently, "put your stockings and shoes back on and I'll buy you a 'Buster' at Paddy's Market, on our way home, that'll put the colour back into your cheeks."

It was getting late by the time they arrived at the market and the smell of hot chips and peas cooking over the open fires of the Buster sellers filled the air. It was a favourite meal with the mill workers, hot and filling and cheap.

"Two please," Billy asked, paying his money to the crone who piled their chips onto cracked plates and topped them with a ladle full of peas from a huge pot bubbling over the fire. They found a place to sit on the wooden benches around the fire and gorged on the feast with their fingers.

"Are you happy Nancy?" Billy asked.

Nancy nodded. "I've never been more so," she said softly.

"Nor me." For a moment, Nancy thought he was going to kiss her right there and then, amongst the diners at the Buster Stall.

"What's his problem?"

Nancy pulled back.

"Who's?"

"You know who," Billy continued. "Your father. What's his problem?"

Nancy grimaced, feeling a pang of guilt at her flirtatious behaviour towards Joe. "He's just a bit overprotective, that's all."

Billy stood up and returned their plates to the crone.

"Are you sure that's all?" he said, leading her away from the heat and towards Castle Street.

Nancy felt her heart begin to thump. Joe's wrath, if he found out she'd been seeing Billy, didn't bear thinking about.

She took a deep breath. "He says he'll kill any man who comes near me."

There, she'd said it. She waited for Billy's reaction.

"Does he now," he said thoughtfully, "and what about you, Nancy, what do you want?"

Nancy stopped and faced him. "YOU, Billy Donnelly," she said from her heart. "YOU."

Billy smiled a slow and warm smile, his dark brown eyes glowing and darkening with desire for her.

"Then there's nothing and nobody else that matters," he said, taking her arm and linking it into his.

It was late when Billy kissed Nancy goodnight at the end of the close leading to her home. "I'll meet you from work on Friday," he whispered, "we need to talk about things more."

"More?" Nancy asked. "About what?"

"Our future, Nancy Cassiday," Billy replied, kissing her again, "our future."

Nancy felt a rush of love for Billy almost overwhelm her. *He'd stand up to Joe alright* she told herself. *Billy could do anything.*

"Till Friday," Billy whispered, "at Baxters gate."

Nancy felt as though she were floating till she saw Agnes's face and her feet returned to earth with a thump.

"You look as thou' you've had a good time then," Agnes smirked.

"I said not to wait up for me," Nancy returned, "but seeing as how you've mentioned it, YES, I have had a good time."

"Then you'd better make the most o' it, 'cause when Joe comes home it'll be no more MR DONNELLY."

Nancy flinched. "Don't count on it Agnes, like I said, it's not in your best interests to tell Joe anything."

Agnes eyes narrowed. "Think you're clever do you, Miss High and Mighty, well just remember, everythin' comes to them that waits and I can bide my time, Nancy Cassiday, I can bide my time."

Nancy coloured. She didn't want Agnes as an enemy, not now, it was enough having to deal with Joe and his madness.

"STOP IT Agnes!" she cried. "I'm not your enemy. I'm your friend, if you'll let me."

Agnes laughter cackled round the small kitchen.

"FRIEND!" she screeched. "That's a good one, FRIEND!"

She reached into her apron pocket and pulled out a flat, green gin bottle. "THAT," she spat, waving the bottle in Nancy's face, "THAT's the only friend I need."

Nancy drew back in pity and disgust. Was this what Joe's passion for her had done to Agnes?

"That's not the answer Agnes," Nancy said gently, trying to keep the guilt out of her voice for the pain she must have put her through with her childish taunts about Joe.

"Is it no'?" Agnes retorted. "An' what do you ken aboot anythin'?"

She uncorked the bottle and drank the gin straight from the neck, as she made her way to the back room where her sons slept. She'd taken to spending every night there since Joe left, secretly drinking till she found oblivion and often falling into Nancy's bed drunk and incapable.

"And dinna you worry my dearie," she said darkly, before disappearing into the dimness of the back room, "your secret's safe wi' me… FOR NOW."

Chapter 15

Harry Duncan had his head down, boning out a side of beef when Euan MacPherson knocked on the open door of his butcher's shop.

"Be with you in a tick," Harry called, skilfully removing a bone from its covering of muscle and wiping his hands on his apron.

He looked with surprise and a little trepidation as he realised who had knocked.

"Why, Sergeant MacPherson," he smiled weakly. "Goin' the messages today are we, your good lady having a day off?" Harry Duncan's mind was whirling, the police calling into his shop meant only thing...TROUBLE.

Euan saw the look of concern on the butcher's face. "Mrs MacPherson's fine, Harry, and so are you, it's that young lad that works for you I want to have a word with."

Harry peered into the back shop where Robbie Robertson was furiously piling offal into a basin and pretending not to hear what was being said.

"Robbie!" Harry exclaimed. "Whit's he been up to then Sergeant, nothing serious I hope?"

Euan eyed Harry. "I just want a word with him, that's all." Both men stood in silence while Robbie rinsed his hands under the tap and dried them on a cloth, his heart threatening to stop beating through fear. Finally, he came into the front shop and met Euan's eyes.

"Sergeant MacPherson," he breathed hoarsely, "whit's the problem?"

Harry Duncan's eyes widened with interest. Robbie had been up to something, that was for sure, but Euan wasn't about to give him the pleasure of hearing about it.

"A little privacy, Harry, if you please, what I have to say to Robbie is for his ears only."

"We could go out the back onto Todburn Lane, if you want," Robbie stuttered, "there's nobody aboot at this time of the day," He could feel his knees buckling. Lexie must have told her father what he'd done to her and now there was no escaping the long arm of the law.

Euan followed the lad up the well-worn steps out onto the lane and sat him down on the stone dyke.

"I suppose you know why I'm here Robbie?" he asked sternly, his hands clasped behind his back and his feet firmly planted on the cobbled road.

Robbie nodded dumbly, his eyes fixed on a clump of weeds growing out of the cassies.

"And, what have you got to say for yourself?"

Like a cornered rat, Robbie sought an escape route. "It was all Lexie's idea," he blurted out. "She wanted to…"

Euan shook his head and held up a stopping hand. "Now Robbie, just admit you were wrong and we'll forget all about it."

Robbie could hardly believe his ears. "I was wrong?" he repeated querulously, not really knowing what he was admitting to. "I'm very sorry, Sergeant MacPherson, very sorry."

Euan felt a stab of sympathy for the lad, he remembered his own first love but asking and expecting Lexie to marry him at her age was a stretch too far.

He took the silver ring out of his tunic pocket. "So, I'm returning this to you and if I ever catch you as much as looking at Lexie again, I won't be so easy on you the next time. Do you understand me?"

Robbie stared at the ring in stunned silence. The proposal, he was talking about the proposal. He felt the weight of the world drop from his shoulders. "Right, Sergeant MacPherson," he mumbled, acutely aware of the lucky escape he'd had. "She'll never see me again… I promise."

"Well, see that you keep your word and Robbie… if I find oot you've been hanging around her again, you know what'll happen!"

Happy that he'd cleared the problem up, Euan MacPherson, nodded and turned on his heel. He'd have no more trouble from that young buck. He chuckled. Annie could rest easy, no harm had been done and Lexie would soon get over her dose of puppy love.

Robbie gazed at the ring till Harry Duncan's voice brought him back to reality.

"If you want to keep your joab, Mr Robertson, get yourself back to work. The black puddin' isn't goin' to make itself."

He'd loved Lexie, that was for sure and he'd loved how it felt to be the first to have her. Now that he had made her his, no one would want to have her, he reasoned, a smile returning to his face. She may not want him now, but once he let it be known what she'd let him do to her, her reputation would be in shreds and then, she'd come running back to him, just wait and see.

"Comin' Mr Duncan," he called back, almost skipping down the steps, inhaling the smells of blood and offal as he tipped the heavy basin into the cooking pot.

"And what was all that aboot?" Harry Duncan questioned. "You got yourself into trouble?"

"No Mr Duncan," Robbie grinned, "no trouble at all."

Lexie fell into step with Sarah the next morning as they headed to school. Sarah had been right, Robbie Robertson was a pig and so was his little brother Davie.

Sarah sensed something was wrong. Lexie's bouncy manner was missing.

"How's the engagement going?" she asked, not sure if she wanted to hear the answer, especially if it involved Baxters Park and Davie Robertson. She shuddered at the thought.

"Engagement?" Lexie said airily. "What engagement?"

Sarah stopped in her tracks and grabbed Lexie's left hand. "Your ring," she gasped, "have you lost it?"

Lexie pulled her hand free. "Don't be daft, I've broken things off."

Sarah blinked. "But…"

"Yes, I know," interrupted Lexie. "I still love him a bit, but I've decided not to marry him. I'm going to finish school and see your dad about working at the weaving in Baxters."

It was all very matter of fact and took Sarah completely off balance. "But, I thought he was the only man you'd ever love and…"

"You are a complete idiot Sarah, and you know so little about boys, so how could you understand that it's a woman's pro-ogative, or something, to change her mind."

Sarah's eyes narrowed. "You mean prerogative." Something didn't ring true, just two days ago, Lexie was swearing undying love for Robbie and now...

The school bell sounded and they quickened their step.

"I'll see you later," called Lexie, hurrying through the school door, ensuring that no more awkward questions were posed. She'd tell Sarah all about her change of heart later but not about the reason why. That secret, she would take to the grave.

When Euan had come home that evening, Annie was relieved to hear the news about Robbie Robertson and that the engagement, as it was, was now off and off for good.

"Are you sure he understands?" she asked, finding it hard to believe things had gone so well. "Ssshhhh now, Annie, the lad's been told and we'll have no more trouble from him."

"And Lexie," Annie queried, "is she over him, do you think?"

"Absolutely." He patted her shoulders and kissed her forehead. "Now, let's hear no more about it. She's a growing girl and she's a good girl too, so stop worrying."

Annie had tossed and turned all night, remembering vividly her own feelings towards her first love, Billy Dawson and how she'd willingly submitted to his demands and the result of that coupling, was now living in Belfast with his adoptive parents.

Her thoughts turned to Bella, her only friend in the poorhouse where she'd given birth to Billy's son and her only way of knowing how and where he was. She must write to Bella soon, let her know how things were and get her to bring her up to date with her son's life. Since Alex Melville's death, she'd hardly been in touch with Bella, but now maybe the time was right. Lexie was almost old enough to know that she had a half brother who she hoped would also want to hear he had a half sister.

Annie had watched Lexie the following day at the breakfast table, and the fear she saw in the daughter's eyes two days ago, seemed to have gone. Perhaps Euan was right, it was just a case of puppy love, now over, and never to be spoken off again.

"Have a good day at school Lexie," she called as her daughter rushed out of the door.

Everything's going to be alright, Annie told herself as she found pen and paper in the bureau drawer and sat down to write to Bella.

Chapter 16

Joe's tour with the Concert Party was going well. His singing was clapped and cheered at every venue and he wrote every week to Nancy, telling her of his successes. He always asked her to pass on his regards to Agnes and their children, but the main thrust of his letters were always directed to Nancy. Nothing sexual, he knew how much he had to control that side of himself, but always praising her dark Irish beauty and saying how much he missed seeing her and how he was looking forward to coming home at the end of June. But, when Nancy read between the lines, there was always the veiled reference to Billy Donnelly and his thieving family, who Nancy should avoid at all costs.

She showed Joe's latest letter to Billy. "He's mad!" she exclaimed fearfully, "I don't know what he'll do if he finds out we're still together."

Billy gathered her into his arms. "Now, now, Nancy," he told her, "we both know that sooner or later he's going to have to realise he can't keep you at home forever and that I'm the one you love and are going to marry."

Nancy pulled back, her eyes shining with renewed hope. "Will we really get married Billy?" she asked.

He pulled her into his arms again. "Of course we will, and the sooner the better."

The weeks running up to Joe's return passed in blissful denial as Nancy and Billy drew closer together. Thoughts of his temper were blocked from Billy's mind on their weekly Saturday nights at the dancing, as Billy waltzed Nancy round the floor, tightening his grip on her waist at the end of each dance, making sure she knew how much he wanted her and gripping her hand in his as he walked her home at the end of the night.

"He'll be back home soon," Nancy announced dismally the first Saturday in June, gazing into Billy's eyes for reassurance that everything would be alright.

"I know," Billy whispered, "I know," remembering his last encounter with Joe Cassiday and the strange look in his eye as he squared up to the younger man. "I'll sort something out," he said, pulling her towards him and feeling the warmth of her body pressing against him. He wasn't quite sure how he'd sort things out, but the closeness of Nancy convinced him that he would, or die in the attempt.

They moved further into the shadows of the close till they reached Agnes's door.

The house was in darkness.

"Looks like Agnes has gone to bed," Billy said trying to prolong his time with Nancy. "Maybe you could make me some tea before the long walk back to Lochee."

Nancy hesitated. "You mean… come in?"

Billy nodded. "Just for a little while," he urged, "and just one cup."

Nancy frowned. "She's a light sleeper Billy and I don't know…"

Billy placed a silencing finger on her lips. "We won't make a sound," he whispered, "after all this may be the last time I see you for a while, once 'you know who' returns."

The heat was building in Billy and he knew it would take more than tea to quench it. His desire for Nancy had been deepening inside him for weeks now and with Joe's control over her, it may be his last chance to prove his love for her, before he had to face up to the reality of how he would deal with the man.

The urgency in Billy's kisses was rapidly overcoming Nancy's fear and with a shy smile she gently unlocked the door. The smell of alcohol and smoke from Agnes's clay pipe filled the small lobby as they tiptoed into the kitchen. "She's been at the drink again," mouthed Nancy, gaining confidence that Agnes wouldn't be awake till the 'knocker up' tapped on the back room window, signalling to the dwellers that it was 'six o'clock and all's well'.

Nancy poked the fire and added some coal from the bunker. "That'll be enough light to see by," she whispered, as she swung the black iron kettle over the heat to boil.

Billy sat down in Joe's chair and pulled her onto his knee. "Now, isn't this better than standing outside in the close?" he asked, his true intention already firmly fixed in his head.

Nancy nodded mutely in agreement, not sure about anything, but as he tipped her head down towards him his lips found hers again and again. Wordlessly, he slowly stroked her hair, her arms, her hips, then gently he began pushing her dress further and further up over her thighs, until he found what he was searching for.

Nancy felt unable to resist, following an instinct that seemed to have arisen from nowhere, she found herself open up to Billy, emotionally as well as physically. Forgetting the kettle now steaming over the coals and the need for silence, they both slid from the chair onto the rag run in front of the fire.

Time seemed to stop as Billy pushed aside her clothing, kissing and stroking the soft flesh beneath. Her scream came from somewhere deep in her soul, as Billy found his way inside her, her nails digging into his back with every thrust.

His love for her had turned into lust and there was no stopping either of them now as the heat from their bodies and from the fire mingled into his sweat and her tears.

Neither of them heard the room door open, nor the soft footfall approach their tangled bodies, but it was a cool breeze of air through the open door that alerted Nancy to the presence of Agnes.

A wave of horror washed over her, obliterating in a moment the sensual pleasure she had just experienced with Billy and replacing it with fear and shame. She pushed Billy onto his side in her haste to cover herself.

"What's wrong?" he asked, blinking at Nancy, who was suddenly on her feet.

He followed her eyes to the figure standing behind him, the firelight casting shadows on Agnes's already hollow face, now laced with a sneer.

"Time you went back to Lochee, where you belong," she spat.

Billy looked at the crone through the shadows. "Hello again, Agnes," he said quietly, taking in for the first time the plainness of the woman and beginning to understand Joe's possessiveness of Nancy, as he buttoned his trousers and tried to regain the upper hand.

"And you'd better not darken this door again, if you know what's good for you."

They held eye contact till Nancy broke through the hostility.

"Please go, Billy," she whispered. "It'll be alright." Her hand tightened on his arm. "Please!"

"If you say so, Nancy," he said quietly "but not because she's told me to."

Nancy was shaking now. The small kitchen that had been so hot a few minutes ago, now felt freezing. "Everything'll be fine," she kept repeating as she steered Billy out the door and back into the darkness of the close, but she knew in her heart, nothing would be fine again, not if Agnes had anything to do with it.

"Are you sure you'll be alright?" Billy asked, concern now replacing the lust.

Nancy could feel tears forming behind her eyelids and fear beginning to gnaw at her gut. She nodded. "You'd best go," she murmured. "I love you."

Billy gazed at her. "And, I love you too," he said, meaning every word, "and everything will be alright," he told her. "I'll make sure it is."

With a confidence he didn't feel, he kissed her gently on the cheek and began his long walk home to Lochee. The enormity of what they'd done now sat heavily on his young shoulders as he plodded through the night. They were in love with one another, that was certain, but what they did was definitely a sin. Tomorrow he would go to confession and ask absolution from Father Monaghan, but even as he contemplated his Catholic punishment, he knew that he would do the same again, given half a chance.

Agnes had made a pot of tea and was pouring herself a cup when Nancy came back into the kitchen.

"Is there any tea for me?" she asked meekly, knowing she would have to use all her wiles to get into Agnes's good books and maintain her secret when Joe came home.

"No," came the short reply, as Agnes pushed tobacco into her pipe and lit it with a taper from the fire.

"We're going to be married Agnes," Nancy began, "and then I'll be out of your hair for good, but..."

Agnes puffed on her pipe. "But?" she said. "But what? If I tell Joe that would spoil your little game, would it?"

Nancy hunched her body nearer to the fire, her face turned away from Agnes.

"What do you want from me," she asked, "to keep you from telling Joe about tonight?"

Agnes smirked to herself. At last, she had sweet, beautiful, desirable

Nancy just where she wanted her. Beholding to her, forever.

"I don't know yet," she retorted, tapping the remains from the pipe into the grate. "And when I do," she continued, standing up and drinking the last of her tea, "you'll be the first to know." Then she tapped the side of her nose with her finger. "No," she grinned, making Nancy look at her for the first time, "you'll be the second to know."

In the silence that followed, Agnes turned away and returned to the back room, closing the door quietly behind her. For once in her life, she felt in control of her destiny and she wasn't going to relinquish that pleasure any time soon.

Chapter 17

The episode with Robbie Robertson was fading from Lexie's mind as her thoughts turned to leaving school and starting work in Baxters as a weaver.

Euan had said he'd dealt with things and as far as she was concerned, Robbie Robertson was now history.

"Can I go and see Sarah's dad soon?" she begged Annie. "Mr Dawson's in charge at Baxters and he knows I'm a clever girl and I'll pick up the weaving fast and…"

"Hush up now Lexie, for just a minute." Her mother held up her hand to silence her daughter. Lexie was born long after Annie's love for Billy Dawson had happened and knew nothing of the past. She also didn't know that Billy had fathered Annie's first born son in Ireland, nor did Billy for that matter. Annie nearly told him at Mary's funeral, but Josie McIntyre had been in the picture then and, eventually, Billy had married her when she became pregnant with Sarah, their first born, and now, Lexie's best friend.

"Why are you so keen to work at the mill, Lexie?" she asked her daughter, not for the first time. "It's not as great as you seem to think it is and there's no future in it."

Lexie crossed her arms in the huff. "Well, it was good enough for you wasn't it, so why can't it be good enough for me?"

Annie took a deep breath. "Times have changed Lexie. I didn't have any choice back then. It was work or want and I did what I could just to survive."

She stroked her daughter's fair hair. *Just like her father's*, she thought, remembering Alex Melville, the man who had promised so much happiness but delivered nothing but hurt, apart from Lexie that is, her beautiful, feisty, brave daughter.

"Look, if you really want to work in the mill, I'll go and see Mr Dawson and ask him about you learning the weaving."

Lexie's eyes lit up. "Will you really?" she gasped, hugging Annie tightly. "Thanks Mum," she continued breathlessly, "you're the best."

Annie extricated herself from her daughter's grip. "Now, get on with your homework before Euan gets in and leave it with me."

Annie was over Billy and any feelings she had for him, but it was still going to be difficult to speak to him about Lexie, especially with Josie still resentful about their past. Maybe it would be better to see him at the mill, rather than at home, she considered, but see him she must. He would surely understand Annie's desire to steer her daughter away from becoming a mill worker and perhaps talk her into something different, although what exactly, she didn't know.

The next day, she presented herself at the lodge keeper's wooden hut at Baxters mill gate.

"Well," said the keeper, "an' whut brings you back here?" he asked, eyeing Annie with a mixture of confusion and curiosity. Annie searched into her bag and produced a small envelope. "Could you see that Mr Dawson gets this, please?" she asked. "I'll wait," she added.

The gateman frowned. "You mean you want it taken to 'im now?"

Annie nodded. "Please," she repeated.

"You realise this isn't usual, during workin' hours an all?"

Annie smiled and pressed a shilling into his hand. "Just this once," she said sweetly, "for old times' sake."

The gateman popped the shilling into his waistcoat pocket. "Wait here."

Annie looked round the tiny wooden hut and remembered the first time she'd been at the mill, looking for work. Mr Campbell had been the mill manager then and had taken her on to be trained as a weaver by Jessie Greig. Jessie had became her best friend in the whole world then and stood by her when no one else did.

But hard work and poverty had taken her at fifty-two. Crippled by a stroke, she'd died at home with her husband and sons about her.

Annie shook the memory from her head. Things had changed for the better for her but not for Jessie and many women like her.

The door clicked open, bringing her thoughts back to today. "Mr Dawson says you've to come up to the office straight away," the lodge keeper said, handing her back the envelope. "Do you mind the way?"

"I do," she replied, "how could I forget it?"

Billy Dawson's name and title, 'Manager', were etched into the brass plate on the outside of the door. Taking a deep breath, Annie knocked.

"Come in."

Billy sat behind the same desk Mr Campbell had sat at and stood up as Annie entered. Annie could feel the awkwardness between them, but Lexie's future was at stake now.

"Billy," she said, "thanks for seeing me."

Billy watched her every move as she sat down, smoothing her skirt and straightening her jacket as she did so.

"Did you think I wouldn't?" he asked.

Annie shook her head. "I just hoped you would," she said softly, "I need your help with Lexie."

"Lexie!" Billy exclaimed. He hadn't known what to expect when he read Annie's note, but didn't expect it to be about Lexie.

His mind raced back to his conversations with Josie about Lexie and how she was a bad influence on Sarah, but...

Billy leant back in his chair. Annie was over forty years of age now, but that gentleness that had first attracted him was still there and her looks had withstood the test of time. If anything, he thought, she'd grown lovelier with the years.

Annie sighed. "She wants to become a weaver," she stated, "and I don't want her working at the mill, Billy, not now, not ever."

Billy kept his eyes fixed on Annie. "Surely, it's quite normal for a young girl to want to be like her mother?"

Annie's lips tightened. "She only wants to be a weaver because she thinks it's grown up and she's growing up fast Billy. Soon, I won't be able to control her at all." Anxiety made her lean forward, her arms bracing her as she felt a lump forming in her throat. "I'm worried for her."

"Is that all there is to it?" Billy now remembered his talk with his own daughter and how Lexie had asked her to meet up with boys in the park.

Annie sat back, her shoulders rounded and her head bent. "She's easily led," she whispered, "and God knows what influence she'll come under working on the weaving flat."

"You mean she might meet a Joe Cassiday!"

Annie flinched, remembering how Joe had swept her off her feet and how angry Billy had been when he found out.

She looked at his handsome face, those deep brown eyes and dark hair just showing signs of grey, looking for signs of an apology. There had been no need to bring the past up like that, but there was no apology forthcoming.

"I think I'm wasting my time," Annie muttered, standing up and turning to go.

"Sit down, Annie," Billy said, realising how much he still hurt and how he had wished it had all been different. The apology came. "I'm sorry Annie," he said, his voice low and hoarse. "Of course, I'll help, but maybe the universe itself has found a way out for you."

Annie sat back down, her brows forming a confused frown.

"Even if I wanted to, I couldn't take Lexie on as a weaver. There's rumours and talk about big money problems in America. The money men there have stopped trading and businesses are closing all over the country." He took out a pack of cigarettes and lit one, blowing the smoke into the air, before continuing," and the problems are spreading over here. Orders for jute are thinning fast and we'll be lucky if we can keep the weavers we've got going, so the answer would have been 'no' anyway."

Annie stared at Billy. "What does that mean for us?" she asked shocked at Billy's words. "For Lexie and Nancy and girls like them?"

"Who knows, Annie... who knows?"

The silence filled the space between them as each became lost in their own thoughts for the future.

"Tell her to come a' see me next Monday," Billy announced, breaking the ice that was forming around Annie and standing up. "I'll see what I can do about getting her into the mill office to help Mrs Fyffe with the paperwork. She's a smart girl Annie and, who knows? She may even get to like it."

Annie's eyes filled with tears of gratitude, her hand extended to Billy. "Thanks Billy, I won't forget this."

Billy took her hand and walked her to his office door, holding it tighter than necessary. "Do you ever think about the old country?" he suddenly asked. "You know, how things were back then?"

Annie felt colour rush to her cheeks as visions of the poorhouse crowded into her head and Billy's son being born into that terrible place of which Billy knew nothing.

"Never," she stated, pulling her hand free. "Lexie will be here at nine o'clock on Monday," she said firmly, turning away and walking back down the passage way on jelly legs.

Billy watched her go. So much water under the bridge, he felt empty, but still, still...

He closed his office door and called Mrs Fyffe on the mill phone.

"Amy," he said when she answered, "can you make yourself available next Monday around nine o'clock?" he asked. "There's a young lass will be coming in looking for work and I think she'd be a great help to you with your filing and stuff. Her name's Lexie Melville." Maybe he could do no more for Annie, but now there was Lexie to look after. He lit another cigarette and considered how he'd put this new development to Josie. She wouldn't be happy, he knew that for sure.

It was a long walk from Baxters Mill to Annie's home in Albert Street, but the fresh air helped to calm her nerves and steady her legs. How could Billy bring up the past and just like that, as she was going out of the door? All the way up King Street and Princess Street her thoughts fought for attention between Lexie and her son in Ireland, but most of all, about Billy. Wasn't that all over with long, long ago? And there was lovely Euan, kind and thoughtful and a wonderful husband and father to their son Ian and step father to Annie's daughter Lexie.

It was a relief to eventually turn into the close and get home. Lexie would be out of school soon and she wanted to use just the right words to guide her into the future.

She made some tea and sliced the fruit cake she'd baked the day before. It was Lexie's favourite. "Ian," she called to her young son, lost in a book in his room, "can you run a message for me?"

The rumble of Ian's feet thundered to a halt at the kitchen door. His smile was as broad as his dad's and Annie chided herself for even thinking about Billy Dawson's brown eyes. "Will you go to Auntie Isobella at the Salvation Army Hall and give her these baby clothes I've knitted for Mrs Kelly's little ones." Ian took the brown paper parcel and tucked it under his arm.

"Who's the fruit cake for?" he asked, spying the rich slices on the plate.

Annie laughed. "For you, of course, but only after you've delivered the parcel."

Ian almost knocked Lexie over as he rushed out the door.

"Where's the fire?" she asked her mother over her shoulder, dropping her books and hanging her coat up on the hallstand

"Oh, you know your brother, Lexie, always in a hurry about something."

Annie busied herself with the tea and cake. "Come," she said, "sit down with your mum, I've got news for you."

Lexie glowed with anticipation. "You've seen him, haven't you and he's going to take me on at the weaving!"

Annie poured the tea. "Yes," she replied, "I've seen Mr Dawson today, now drink your tea and have a slice of fruit cake, then I'll tell you what he's agreed to do for you."

Lexie wolfed down the cake and gulped down the hot tea, wiping her mouth with the back of her hand. "WELL?"

Annie put her cup down and folded her hands in her lap.

"Mr Dawson wants to see you next Monday morning at nine o'clock."

Lexie yelped with delight. "I knew it!" she exclaimed, "I just knew it!"

"Now calm down now Lexie, there's more."

Lexie sat back down in the chair, her face flushed and a huge grin across her face as Annie began to tell her about America and poor orders at the mill, watching anxiously as the grin turned into a thin line.

"So," she continued, "Mr Dawson is going to see about you working in the mill office, just till things pick up," she lied, "then he would consider the weaving again."

Lexie felt her future crumble around her. She'd seen herself as a proud Dundee Weaver, making good money and having her own life, without Robbie Robertson or his ilk, but now, they wanted her to be a silly office girl, no more than a child being told what to do. She felt the tears roll down her young cheeks. Her dream was over even before it had begun.

Chapter 18

Joe's return was imminent, and as the hours dragged towards seven o'clock Nancy became more withdrawn and Agnes more animated.

"Not be long now," she stated, checking the clock for the umpteenth time. "I'm so lookin' forward to seeing him again," she gushed, looking Nancy full in the face. "AREN'T YOU?"

Nancy picked up the iron poker and began raking the coals, sending sparks shooting up the chimney. She had never felt so scared. If Agnes said anything to Joe about her night with Billy, she knew her life with him would be over.

Agnes dug her in the shoulder. "Whit's wrong sweetheart?" she grinned. "Cat got your tongue?"

Nancy felt a rush of heat sweeping over her. She dropped the poker in the grate and stood up, face to face with Agnes. "If you say anything Agnes," she breathed, "anything at all about me and Billy, I swear I'll..."

"You'll WHAT, Miss Pretty?" Agnes cut in angrily. "KILL ME!" She pushed Nancy back down on her chair. "And, what makes you think I'm not dead already, ehh?" Nancy flinched.

"I died a long time ago," she spat, thumping her chest with her bony hand, "so you see, Nancy Cassiday, nothin' you can do can hurt me anymore."

Both of them heard the sound of Joe's boots coming along the close at the same time, accompanied by his singing. Nancy's heart was drumming in her chest and her throat felt as if it was closing up. The door opened. Joe Cassiday was home.

He glanced at Agnes and nodded her presence, before his eyes turned to Nancy and his heart leapt.

She was even more beautiful than he remembered. "Is there any tea Agnes?" he asked without looking at her, "I've a bit of a thirst on me with all that travelling I've been doin'." He dumped his kitbag on the floor.

Agnes filled the kettle and swung it over the fire to boil. "It'll be ready in a jiffy, Joe," she smiled, "Nancy was just saying it'll be nice having you back home again, weren't you Nancy?"

Both sets of eyes turned towards her awaiting her reply.

She felt her insides cringe in resentment. So, this was Agnes's game, forcing her to be sweet to Joe, knowing it was tearing her apart.

"I suppose so," she muttered, keeping her eyes on the kettle, remembering the games she used to play with Joe's emotions, making Agnes feel so rejected.

She bitterly regretted it now, but she knew the boot was now on the other foot and Agnes was going to get her revenge, in a big way.

Joe pulled a chair alongside her and tipped her head up, searching her face for more.

"You only suppose so!" he repeated. "Aren't you sure?"

Nancy tried to turn away, but Joe's fingers stayed put, making sure she looked at him. She could hear Agnes moving closer to hear her answer. Nancy fought to control the wave of nausea that had gripped her insides.

"Of course I'm s-s-suure," she stammered, "it's just I'm not feeling too well," she added, closing her eyes and hoping Joe would release his grip and let her be.

He looked at Agnes, his eyes narrowing. "How long has she been ill?" he asked.

Agnes shrugged her shoulders in ignorance. "Don't know Joe," she replied, her voice laced with pretend concern, "she seemed alright a wee while ago."

"I think I'll be alright Joe, once I have a sleep," she blurted out, not wanting to get involved in any more questions and lies. "It's been a long day…" she finished lamely.

Joe's eyes seemed to bore into her very soul as the silence in the little kitchen became deafening. Nancy tried to stand up. "So, I'll just get to bed," she stammered, trying to make her legs move forward. Suddenly, the room began to swim around her and a dense blackness enveloped her. Joe caught her before her head hit the tiled grate and Agnes froze in disbelief, as Joe carried Nancy through to her bedroom.

"Please don't let anything happen to her," he muttered to his god, panic gripping his heart, as he gently placing Nancy on her bed. "Please don't take her like you took her mother."

Joe squeezed Nancy's hand, rubbing her cold skin and willing her eyes to open.

Agnes was the first to hear her groan. "She's comin' round," she announced nervously. "See, Joe, she's only fainted."

Joe blinked back his tears and gazed closer to make sure Nancy was coming round.

"Are you alright?" he asked hoarsely, brushing his hand over her forehead while Agnes shrank back into the shadows, her heart hardening with every beat. She didn't know how she was going to do it, but Joe had to find out about Billy Donnelly soon, very soon.

Nancy pushed herself up onto her elbows. "What happened?" she said, trying to understand how she got to her bed.

"Sssshhhh," Joe whispered. "You fainted," he told her, "that's all, just a faint. Now, just lie quietly and Agnes will make you some tea."

Agnes stiffened, hearing her name. He always made her feel like a servant instead of his wife. "Sure, Joe," she said, her voice flat and without emotion, "anything you say."

Nancy blinked hard as tears threatened to fall and Joe's face blurred in the dimness of the room. "I'm fine now," she stammered, trying to sit up, "just need a little sleep that's all."

She felt his hands push her gently back onto the pillow, as the shadow of Agnes came into the room. "And that's just what to do," he told her, "it's too much excitement I think, but I'm back now and everything will be alright from here on." His eyes were dark with concern as he turned Agnes and the tea away and followed them out of the room, closing the door quietly behind him.

Nancy lay perfectly still, her eyes closed and her breathing shallow. Her hands drifted down over her stomach and her mind filled with fear. She had heard about women becoming pregnant at the first coupling, then 'honeymoon babies' were born exactly nine months later, or more frighteningly, as the gossips would have it, bastards! Although it had been the only time she and Billy had been together, it had been enough and now, the fates had made the decision for her. She had to escape this place and find Billy before it was too late and before Agnes could betray her.

Joe had left early the next morning, cautioning Agnes to look after Nancy and let her sleep as long as she wanted. "And make sure the boys go to school today," he added, 'silently'.

Agnes had felt her heart harden to stone. "And what about me Joe?" she asked. "Am I to remain SILENT as well?"

The closing of the door behind him left her in no doubt. She was going to tell him about his precious Nancy and her Irish lover soon, very soon and see how SILENT he'd be then.

The next day, it only took Nancy a few minutes to push her few belongings into a carpet bag before starting the long walk to Tipperary in Lochee and Billy, but with every step she felt the weight of guilt pressing down on her shoulders and her mind began to fill with all the possibilities of what might happen in the future. None of which were happy.

By the time she'd reached Bell Street and the road to Lochee, her legs were getting weaker and as the walls of the police station reared up in front of her, blackness engulfed her again.

She was distantly aware of strong arms carrying her into the warmth of a brightly lit room and deep voices murmuring all around her.

"She's coming to, Sarge," said one of the voices, becoming clearer now.

Nancy felt her eyes flicker open. "Where am I?"

"It's alright," said a familiar voice, "you're in safe hands now, so just stay still and try to drink some tea."

A cup of warm, sweet tea was placed onto her lips as her head was raised to receive it.

"You're in Bell Street Police Station Nancy. We think you fainted out in the street."

The familiar voice was matched to the familiar face of Euan MacPherson.

"Mr MacPherson," Nancy whispered, "is it you?"

"It is Nancy," he assured her, "and I've sent for your Auntie Annie to come and get you and take you home."

Nancy's eyes widened with fear. "But, Mr MacPherson, I can't go home again... I just CAN'T."

Euan eyed the distressed girl in front of him. Something was badly wrong. "When your Auntie Annie comes, she'll know what's best, so just hush now and get back your strength."

Annie had rushed down to the station as soon as the Euan's Constable gave her the news. All manner of worries flashed through her mind and guilt about not keeping an eye on Mary's daughter clung around her shoulders, tightening her neck and forcing a pain across her eyes.

Breathing rapidly, she almost ran into the police station where Euan stopped her in her tracks. "It's alright Annie," he said, his voice strong and calm, "she's fine. She just fainted in the street." Annie's eyes focused on her husband's calm face.

"Fainted," she repeated, "but where was she going and WHY did she faint? She's a young woman and if she was ill, she would have told me, surely."

"You can ask her that yourself," Euan replied, "she's next door, recovering nicely, but before you go in, I have to say that when I suggested you take her home, she got very agitated, scared even, so go slowly with her Annie, let her come to you in her own time."

Annie was shocked at Nancy's appearance. There was a gauntness around her eyes and a paleness in her lips. Euan was right, this wasn't the happy Nancy she knew. She pulled a chair over to the old leather sofa where she lay and took her hand.

"Whatever it is Nancy," she said, "we'll make it better. Your mum knows that I'll always look after you and now you should know it as well."

The warmth of Annie's concern found its mark in Nancy's heart and the tears began to flow. The whole story of Joe's obsession and her love for Billy Donnelly came out. "And now," she whispered, "I'm going to have Billy's child." She turned her eyes to Annie, pleading for understanding and Annie knew only too well, what her niece was feeling. The past flooded in again, washing over her like water over stones as she was delivered of Billy's son in the poorhouse. And now, history looked like repeating itself, only this time, she would make sure Nancy's child didn't suffer the same fate as had her own.

Chapter 19

Amy Fyffe knew her stuff. She'd run the mill office for over twenty years and had met and found a way through to all types who had crossed her path, but nothing had prepared her for the rough diamond that was Lexie Melville.

"So, it's Lexie, is it?" she smiled. "Mr Dawson says you're going to be helping me in the office for a while, is that right?"

Lexie shrugged her shoulders, taking in the dark wood panelling and frosted glass that surrounded her. "Suppose so."

The smile on Mrs Fyffe's face faded a little.

"So tell me, what do you think about office work Lexie, is it something that you think you'd like to do, say filing or typing maybe?"

"Can't file," came the sullen reply, "and can't type, so…"

Amy Fyffe realised very quickly that Lexie was going to be a handful, but in her mind, the answer to everything was to keep busy and that's just what she expected Lexie to do.

"Right," she said briskly, "that pile of envelopes over there need opening and the contents sorting for distribution to the other offices." She urged Lexie forward towards the table and flipped open an ink pad. "Take this," she said, handing Lexie a rubber date stamp. "First, we open the envelope… carefully, then remove the contents and stamp the date on the top of each letter, like this, think you can do that?"

Lexie's face scrunched up in a look of disgust. This wasn't what she wanted to do at all, she wanted to be a weaver, making her own money and being free from all controls, but here she was stamping the date on stupid letters. It was almost too much to bear but she knew there were no other choices open to her right now.

The day dragged on and then the week, with Mrs Fyffe always finding her something else boring to do. She now envied Sarah's future, going to university and becoming a teacher sounded much better than filing stupid bits of paper in stupid filing cabinets. She almost wished she'd stayed at school.

Her thoughts were interrupted by a brisk Mrs Fyffe. "When you've finished the filing Lexie, please take these prints down to the Drawing Office. Give them to Miss Malvina Edwards, the Drawing Office secretary and wait till she checks them back in. She'll give you a check-in slip to bring back to me."

Lexie picked up the brown envelope and looked inside. Blue pictures of wheels and cogs looked back at her. "Prints," she muttered to herself, "Drawing Office." And where was she supposed to find that?

The painted sign above a set of double doors saying Drawing Office made it easy to find, but what met her eyes when she entered the long room was a whole new world.

All along both sides of the office were men standing at huge flat boards, diligently moving wooden rulers over the surface and drawing, what appeared to Lexie, black lines.

At the far end of the room, sat a woman at a typewriter, who she assumed was Miss Malvina Edwards. Very quietly, she closed and door and started walking toward the far end of the room as twenty pairs of male eyes watched her with interest.

They didn't meet many young girls in this job and this one was quite a looker, or so Charlie Mathieson thought, one of the junior draughtsmen. Yes, quite a looker.

To Lexie's young eyes, Miss Malvina was very, very old and took her time checking the prints before, finally, handing over the receipt. "Now, take this back to Mrs Fyffe immediately," she said sternly, "no dawdling."

Lexie nodded and started the long walk back to the door, but this time, she could see all the faces watching her and one of them was smiling widely at her and mouthing something. It looked like 'see you later', but Lexie couldn't be sure. She felt her face redden as she left the room. Maybe working at Baxters Office wasn't going to be so bad after all.

She duly returned the check-in slip to Mrs Fyffe. "Anything else?" she asked sweetly.

Amy Fyffe eyed her young charge. "Well, if you're offering," she said, wondering what had brought about the change in Lexie's attitude, "maybe you could file those invoices for me?"

Without a word of protest, Lexie nodded and bent to the task. Amy Fyffe smiled to herself. Her plan was working, keeping Lexie busy was plainly the way forward and she'd be able to report to Mr Dawson on Monday that Lexie had been 'tamed'.

A long queue had formed at the tram stop in Princes Street by the time Lexie had gathered her coat and bag and made her way out of Baxters Office and up King Street. She usually walked home, but this time she decided to treat herself as a reward to all her hard work.

"Going my way?" said a male voice over her shoulder. Lexie turned quickly to find Charlie Mathieson grinning at her from ear to ear. Colour raced to her cheeks again.

"Maybe," she said coyly.

The tram clattered to a stop and the queue moved forward. Lexie felt her arm being held as she stepped onto the platform. "Allow me," Charlie smiled, as he steered her to the back of the tram and sat down beside her.

"I'm Charlie, by the way, Charlie Mathieson." He extended a hand out to her, but Lexie didn't respond, for the first time in her life she couldn't think of a thing to say or do. "I saw you today in the Drawing Office," he continued unabashed, "as did every other man," he added, nudging her gently. "You're new aren't you?"

Lexie nodded, still unable to find her voice.

"And, do you have a name?"

What was wrong with her? This was something new to her, not being able to speak up for herself. She had entered the world of men and didn't know how to behave around them. Sure, she could wrap Euan round her little finger and even Robbie Robertson hadn't left her speechless, but Charlie Mathieson...

As the tram trundled up into Albert Street, Charlie got up. "Well, this is my stop. It's been a pleasure... Miss?"

At last Lexie was able to raise her eyes to meet his. "Lexie," she said. "My name, it's Lexie."

Charlie's grin returned, wider than ever. "See you later... Lexie." He winked as he strode up the tram and jumped off, turning to wave at her as the tram went past.

Lexie almost missed her stop as her mind raced around in circles and she relived the last few minutes of her encounter with Charlie Mathieson. Something had changed, she didn't know exactly what, but she felt different about herself... about everything. No longer a little girl, Lexie suddenly felt very grown up. A real man had made it clear he liked her and Lexie couldn't wait till Monday to see him again.

On returning home, her grown-up mood quickly evaporated as her mother met her in the hallway and guided her into the kitchen. "Sit down, Lexie," Annie instructed, her face creased with worry. "Something has happened and I need your help."

Lexie's eyes widened. "What is it?" she asked. "Where's Euan? What's happened?"

Annie held her finger up to her lips. "Sssshhhh," she whispered. "Nancy'll hear you."

"Nancy!" Lexie repeated. "She's here?"

Annie nodded. "She's not well Lexie and we need to look after her for a little while, till she's better."

Lexie relaxed a little. Euan was OK and nobody had died, so whatever it was that was wrong with Nancy, she could cope with it. The grown-up feeling returned.

Annie took her daughter's hands in hers. "She has nowhere to go," she explained, "so she's going to stay with us for a little while, but that'll mean you sharing your room with her Lexie... can you do that?"

The child in Lexie returned. "But, WHY ME?" she wailed. "Why can't she share with Ian? His room's bigger than mine." She could feel tears of selfish frustration burning in her eyes; she'd been having a lovely day and now this...

Annie tightened her grasp on Lexie's hands. "She can't share with Ian," she said gently, "because she's going to have a bairn."

The room fell silent as the news sank in. "But, she can't be having a bairn, she's not married or anything..." Lexie's voice tailed off as she realised the truth. Nancy was a 'fallen woman.' She'd heard about 'fallen women' and what happened to them and her young mind closed in shame.

Annie sensed her daughter's withdrawal and let go of Lexie's hands. "She's my niece Lexie and your Auntie Mary's daughter," she said firmly, "and I won't see her on the streets. She'll be staying with us and sharing your room for as long as she needs to, I hope, with your agreement."

Lexie hung her head. She liked Nancy and had always wished she'd been more like her with her dark eyes and hair, but now... her mind went back to her encounter with Robbie Robertson in the park and the memory of how he had forced himself inside her. How easily could this have happened to her! What if it had, she wondered, what would she have done if Robbie Robertson had given her a baby?

Somewhere inside her, compassion stirred and the unfairness of the grown-up world crowded in. She turned her blue eyes onto her mother and nodded.

"Thanks Lexie," Annie whispered, as she feared history repeating itself in the shape of Nancy and prayed that the same fate wouldn't await her own daughter.

Chapter 20

"Where is she?" Joe repeated for the umpteenth time, his voice hardening with every repetition.

"I told you Joe," Agnes whinged, "she must have left after I went to work this morning and I'm sure she'll be back soon..."

Joe's eyes narrowed as Agnes bent quickly to sweep the hearth and put more coal on the fire.

"She'd better be," he said, the harshness in his voice making Agnes cringe. "And, she'd better not have gone anywhere near that layabout, Donnelly," he added, his anxiety turning to anger at the thought of what might have happened during his three months on tour with the Concert Party.

He leaned over to Agnes and gripped her arm. "But, you wouldn't have let him anywhere near now would you!" It was more a statement than question and Agnes felt herself crumble under his gaze. "WOULD YOU?" he yelled.

Agnes began to shake and tears spilled down her hollow cheeks. "I tried to stop him Joe, I really did, but..."

Joe could feel white hot anger surging through his veins. He hauled Agnes to her feet, both hands now gripping her arms so tightly she almost screamed. "BUT!" he roared. "BUT WHAT?"

Agnes tried to pull away from his grasp but he only tightened it further. "TELL ME."

"She let him in while I was asleep in the next room," she stammered, "but it was only the once Joe and he never came again, I promise you, he never…"

Joe released his grip and Agnes fell to the floor, her sobbing now uncontrolled.

So, this was it, his worse fears realised, Nancy and Billy Donnelly. His fists clenched so tightly the nails drew blood. And now, there was only one way out for Mr Donnelly he reasoned, and that was death. He'd find him and kill him.

Euan MacPherson was off duty when he called at Cox's Mill looking for Billy Donnelly. If what Annie had said was true, he had to be found and made to marry Nancy, especially before Joe Cassiday found out and tracked him down.

The mill manager, Andrew Mackay, had been at school with Euan and welcomed him warmly into his office.

"Well, well, Euan MacPherson," he smiled, "and what brings you here, not looking for work, I take it?"

Euan sat down and sighed. "I only wish it was for that reason, but it's about a more personal matter."

"Go on," urged Andrew Mackay, "there's nothing you can tell me that will go beyond those doors."

Euan took a deep breath, "it's about one of your workers, a spinner, name of Billy Donnelly."

"Donnelly!" exclaimed Andrew. "Fine young lad if I remember correctly. His father had a bit of bother a while ago, but you'll probably know about that, being in the police and all."

Euan nodded. "Sorry business that, I well remember him and his poor mother visiting his dad in the cells the day after his arrest. And, I agree with you, he seemed a sensible enough lad, but I'm afraid he's got a young lassie into a bit of bother and that's why I need to speak with him."

Andrew Mackay sat back in his chair, his eyebrows drawing together with concern.

"I take it you mean… in the family way?"

"Her name's Nancy Cassiday and she's my wife's niece."

Andrew MacKay flinched. "I'll send the lodge keeper to fetch him here. You can speak to him privately for as long as you need to and I just hope things work out for all concerned."

The men shook hands and Euan was left on his own to ponder how to approach the young man he was about to see.

Annie and he had sat up late into the night after Nancy and Lexie had gone to bed trying to figure out the best way forward.

"She's not a child Annie," Euan had counselled, "and I think telling Billy Donnelly about what's happened is the most we should do, then it's up to her what she does next."

Annie felt her heart sink at the thought of what Nancy would have to face if Billy Donnelly didn't marry her, and quickly. Euan just didn't understand what could happen to a woman alone and with a child to support. He didn't know anything about her own illegitimate son, nor Mary's abortion, and although the war had changed much, it hadn't lessened the shame and distress doled out to women in trouble, especially by other women. And there was Billy Dawson, shouldn't he be told about Nancy? He may have not had much to do with her upbringing but he was her father.

The knock on the door of Mr Mackay's office heralded the arrival of Billy Donnelly. His face was white and his eyes widened with fear when he saw Euan MacPherson.

"Whit's wrong?" he gasped. "Is it my mum, is she OK?"

Euan motioned him to sit down.

"Calm down Billy," Euan said kindly, "your mum's alright and so's your dad."

The fear faded from Billy's eyes and was quickly replaced by confusion.

"But why are you here then?"

"It's about Nancy," Euan began, but before he could go further, Billy jumped up from the chair, his eyes now bright with terror.

"What's he done to her?" he stammered. Again Euan told Billy to sit down.

He eyed the young man warily. This wasn't the reaction he had expected.

"What's who done to her Billy?" he asked.

Billy clenched his fists till the knuckles turned as white as his face.

"Joe Cassiday," he breathed the name with such hate Euan was taken aback.

"Joe Cassiday," he repeated, "isn't that her father?"

Tears began to form in Billy's eyes. "Father," he said, "more like her jailer."

"Jailer!" Euan repeated. "Now that's a strange thing to say."

"He controls everything she does Sergeant MacPherson and he'd like to see me dead."

Billy was confirming everything Nancy had told Annie about Joe's obsessive behaviour and his hatred of any man who was attracted to her, especially Billy Donnelly.

Euan began to feel deep concern for Nancy and Billy. He knew Joe of old. The war had changed him and the loss of a leg at Ypres had almost broken him. But, Mary had loved him and he her till the TB had taken her. But, how had it come to this? Nancy, petrified of her own step father, and enough to run away!

"Nancy's left home." Euan tried again to broach the subject of Nancy's pregnancy. "She fainted outside the police station on her way to find you."

"Fainted!" Billy gasped. "Is she alright? Tell me she's alright." Billy was on his feet again, his hands gripping the lapels of Euan's jacket.

Euan pushed him back down into the chair. "Now, I've told you to calm down," he shouted, his inability to keep things under control disappearing, "so sit still and listen. Nancy's not ill Billy, she's pregnant with your child."

The silence that followed was tangible.

"She's living with me and her Auntie Annie, so she's safe for now, but Billy, it's time for you to be a man and do the right thing by her." Billy seemed frozen to the spot.

The shock seemed to have robbed him of his tongue. "Do you understand me Billy?" Euan asked, softer this time. There was nothing to be gained by shouting at the lad, he reasoned, not while he was in this state.

"She wants to see you Billy."

The bravado of Billy the young Romeo was evaporating into thin air, leaving behind a very scared young man. He loved Nancy, to be sure he did, but becoming a father at eighteen and providing for a wife filled him with dread.

"I can't," he whispered, his voice barely audible. "I can't."

Euan's eyes looked heavenward for guidance.

"I don't think you have a choice, Billy," he said more firmly this time. "Nancy can't face this alone, nor will she, if I have anything to do with it."

"But, what about the priest, how can I tell him I've sinned?" Billy buried his face in his hands. "God will never forgive me."

Euan reached across the removed Billy's hands from his face, forcing him to meet his eyes.

"I don't care," he said, his voice hoarse with anger, "whether God or the Pope or the King of Scotland himself doesn't forgive you. You've got a lovely young girl in trouble and you'll get her out of it, or it will be worst decision you've ever made."

His grip tightened on Billy as he lifted him out of the chair.

"So, get your coat, you're coming with me NOW, to see your future wife."

His face set with determination, Euan marched Billy Donnelly out of the mill and down to the police station at Bell Street.

"Now, sit down there," he said, "till we get a few things straight about being a man."

Billy slumped in the chair.

"Bring some tea," he told the constable on duty, "and make it sweet, this young man's had a bit of a shock."

Nancy sat sipping at a cup of tea while Annie busied herself peeling potatoes at the kitchen sink.

Her mind had been in overdrive since Euan had left for Cox's Mill and she prayed like never before, that Billy Donnelly would do the decent thing. She kept sneaking glances at her niece, concerned at the stillness of her demeanour, as if she was frozen in time. She had been horrified to learn of Joe Cassiday's obsession with Nancy, finding it hard to believe that both she and Mary had once thought him the most wonderful man in the world. She shook her head sadly, if only Mary had lived, things would have been very different.

Annie was lost in her thoughts of the past when the sound of footsteps on the stairs brought her back to the reality of the situation now facing Nancy.

"That'll be Euan," she said gently, "and Billy too, I'm sure."

At the mention of Billy's name, Nancy seemed to come awake.

"Billy?" she whispered. "Here?"

The door opened and Euan's voice called out Annie's name. She hurried into the hallway, hardly daring to hope that Euan had sorted things.

"Someone to see Nancy," he said, pushing Billy forward.

"She's in the kitchen," Annie replied, "through there Billy." She pointed to the kitchen door.

She glanced at Euan, hoping for confirmation that everything was fine, but he couldn't meet her eyes.

Euan led Annie into the living room as Billy went through the door to Nancy and his fate.

"Is everything alright?" Annie whispered, getting concerned now at Euan's silence.

"Sssshhh," he cautioned her, "let's see how it goes."

Euan and Annie sat gazing into the middle-distance, waiting for the door to open and the young couple to enter smiling and happy. Instead, they heard shouting and the slamming of the front door.

Annie jumped to her feet.

"Nancy," she called out, tears of distress for her niece spilling over.

The young girl sat where Annie had left her, the tea now cold in the cup.

"He's gone," she whispered, "to speak with his priest, he said."

"But, he'll be back... won't he?"

Nancy shook her head, her gaze fixing on Annie's face. "No."

"Oh, Nancy," Annie said, "it'll be alright, I'm here and Euan's here, it'll be alright."

She folded her arms around her niece, finding no resistance. *How is Nancy going to get through this?* she thought. But one thing was sure, Annie would be with her every step of the way. Not for Nancy, the fate that befell Annie herself. For a start, Billy Dawson now had to be told about his daughter's plight.

Chapter 21

Joe walked aimlessly for miles, letting the images of Nancy and Billy Donnelly grow in his head till he lost all reason. What had Donnelly done to her, was the question that went unanswered in his soul. If he'd touched her, even kissed her lips, Joe couldn't bear it.

Darkness fell and he found himself on the slopes of the Dundee Law, the lights of the town below increasing as the lamplighters went about their business.

And why had she fainted like she had? Did she really hate him so much that even being in the same room as him caused her to black out? His thoughts turned to Agnes. She knew more than she said, he decided, and tonight he would make her tell him everything.

His leg was hurting badly now, as he reached the Hilltown. A few drinks would help, he reasoned, just enough to get him home. The pub was filled with pipe smoke and the smell of ale as mill workers crowded at the bar, spending their wages on a Friday night before going back to their wives with little left to hand over for food.

"Whiskey," he nodded to the barman. "Make it a double."

The barman obliged and Joe quickly downed the burning liquid. "Another," he said, handing over a shilling.

"In a bit of a hurry are we?" asked the bar tender amiably.

Joe's eyes were black as coal. "What's it to you?"

The barman backed off. "Nothing squire, nothing at all. Another double it is."

The pain was easing and so were Joe's worries about Nancy.

Of course Billy Donnelly wouldn't have touched her, he decided, he'd have known better than to cross Joe Cassiday.

On the way down the Hilltown, Joe passed the Progress Hall. Men and women were pouring in through the doors and the sound of dance music filtered into the street.

Warm from the whiskey, Joe began to hum the tune to himself, at first, then louder and by the time he'd reached the bottom of the Hilltown, his self-confidence was returning. Sure now that Agnes would have nothing to tell him, he turned into Victoria Road and down the William Lane steps to home. Nancy would be home soon, he was now certain, she wouldn't leave old Joe alone in the world, not his Nancy.

But only Agnes sat by the fire, nursing a cup of tea heavily laced with gin.

She had been lulled by the gin and the heat of the fire and didn't hear Joe come into the gloomy kitchen till he was suddenly standing over her.

"Joe!" she exclaimed anxiously. "I didn't hear you come in. Are you hungry, can I get you anything?"

The sight of Agnes chased away any pleasantness the whiskey had brought.

"Where is she, is she home yet?"

Agnes felt herself sober up. "Sheeee's... I don't know Joe, she's not been back all day."

Agnes flinched as Joe's hands landed on her shoulders, his voice low and menacing as he asked the question.

"Tell me what he did... to Nancy... when he was here, and I'll know if you're lying."

Agnes was torn between wanting to tell him about what his precious Nancy had been up to with Billy Donnelly, but fear of the consequences rendered her dumb.

"I don't know anything Joe," she stammered, "I was asleep in the back room. SOUND ASLEEP," she emphasised.

His grip tightened again. "Tell me," he demanded again, "or I'll beat you senseless till you do."

Fear washing through Agnes at the knowledge that Joe, would and could, do just that, made the decision for her.

"Ah'right," she cried, her voice cracking with fear, "he was here one night and I... I heard this noise in the kitchen..."

Joe began to darken deep in his heart. "And then?"

Agnes tried to loosen his grip but couldn't. "Then, I came through here and they were," she looked down at the carpet in front of the fire, "lying there... doing things... dirty things!"

The blow to Joe's emotions was almost physical, as he realised what Agnes meant.

A coldness like ice formed in the pit of his stomach. "Get out of my sight," he spat at Agnes, "and tomorrow, get your arse out of here." He shoved her backwards till she fell.

"Joe," she pleaded, "please, don't say that, I love you Joe."

The door slammed behind him, leaving Agnes a miserable heap on the floor.

"Nancy Cassiday," she cursed, "this was all your fault and you'll pay for this night," she whispered to herself. "Mark my words."

Joe turned into Todburn Lane, almost blind with hurt. Charlie would still be up, his brother was always a night owl, sleeping during the day, and drinking and thinking late into the night. It was Charlie that Joe turned to when he came back from Ypres, one leg blasted to Hell and his confidence shattered, and it was Charlie who got him through the pain and loss till Mary restored his peace of mind with her love.

He knocked at the door. "Open up Charlie," he called, "it's your wee brother Joe."

He waited till he heard the chain released and the key turned in the lock.

Charlie's head came round the side of the door. He'd been asleep in front of the fire and a half empty whiskey bottle sat beside his chair. One look at Joe told him something was very wrong.

After throwing some coal onto the fire and stirring it back into life, Charlie filled two glasses with whiskey and handed one to his brother and waited.

The ensuing wails of despair that came from Joe's mouth were almost too much for Charlie to hear, but he waited till they turned to sobs and then stopped.

He refilled the glasses and handed Joe a dishcloth that had been drying by the fire.

"Here," he said softly, "use this."

Joe wiped his face and blew his nose.

"I won't pretend to know what's wrong," said Charlie, "but whatever it is, I'll be here for you when you need me. Just like always."

Joe's love for Charlie welled up in his heart. His brother never judged him, never told him what to do, but just loved him as a brother should.

"I've got myself into a right state," Joe began, "and I don't know how to get rid of these feelings that I have about it all."

Charlie's eyes narrowed. "I take it there's a woman involved."

Joe's eyes refilled with tears. "It's Nancy," he murmured.

Charlie wasn't sure what Joe meant. Nancy was his stepdaughter.

"I love her Charlie," he stated flatly, shrugging his shoulders. "I can't help it. Every time I'm near her I can barely control the urge to touch her."

Charlie said nothing.

"And now," he could feel the emotions bubbling again, "she's been bedded by a layabout called Billy Donnelly and she's left me."

Charlie flinched. Joe's confession was wrong on so many levels and his concern for his brother mounted. "You need to forget her Joe," Charlie told him. "No good can come of it for either of you. She's Mary's daughter for God's sake."

"Don't say that Charlie, don't you realise I can't forget her, sometimes I wish I could."

Charlie's heart ached for his brother's pain, but his head told him he had to steer him away from the dangerous road he was on.

"So, what's to do Joe?"

A fire had come back into Joe's words. "I've thrown Agnes out and I'm going to find Nancy and bring her back. Make her love me. And, if Billy Donnelly comes anywhere near, I'll kill him Charlie, so help me God I will." Charlie winced. He'd seen Joe in many moods over the years, but this one was the most unstable and frightening.

He stood up and took the empty glass from Joe's hand.

"Go to sleep Joe, use my bed, I never sleep much now and tomorrow, we'll look at it all again in the morning, see things differently maybe. What do you say?"

Joe looked at the clock. It was nearly two in the morning and he suddenly felt drained and lifeless again.

"Thanks Charlie," he said, patting his brother's shoulder as he passed his chair, "for not judging and for the bed."

Charlie stayed awake for the rest of the night and as dawn broke, he pulled on his jacket and slipped out of the house. It wasn't a long walk to Baxters Mill, but Charlie knew that the one person who might talk sense into Joe would be turning up there for the day shift.

At half past six the tall figure of Billy Dawson came into view and Charlie stepped out of the shadows.

Billy stopped abruptly, trying to determine who was at the gate. He came closer.

"Charlie!" he exclaimed. "Charlie Cassiday, is it you?"

Charlie nodded. He hadn't spoken to Billy since Joe's marriage to Mary, but Billy was Nancy's father and he needed to know what had happened, before it was too late for Joe and Nancy.

Sensing something was very wrong, Billy led Charlie through the gates and into his office.

"Sit down man," he began, "you look beat."

"It's about your daughter, Nancy."

Billy leant forward across his desk. "Nancy!" he repeated. He saw her at the mill only last week and she was fine, and although he didn't have much contact with her since his marriage to Josie, he always felt she was safe enough with Joe Cassiday looking out for her.

Billy waited, tension mounting in his mind. "What about Nancy?" he asked quietly.

His voice hoarse with emotion, Charlie told Billy the story.

"Where is Nancy now?" he asked.

Charlie raised his shoulders. "I don't know."

"And Joe," Billy asked through clenched teeth, "where's he?"

Charlie looked at Billy, trying to gauge his temper, knowing he was the only one who could deal with Joe. "He's with me at my place on Dens Brae."

Billy stood up. "Then we'd better go see him," he said, the tone of his voice brooking no argument from Charlie.

The two men strode quickly up Dens Brae and into Charlie's dingy kitchen.

Charlie nodded to the door into the other room. "I left him in there, sleeping off the whiskey."

"Wake him up Charlie," Billy instructed firmly, "we need to get to the bottom of this and find Nancy."

Charlie disappeared into the darkness of the other room, but returned alone.

Joe had gone.

Chapter 22

Lexie dressed in the darkness of her room, conscious of Nancy curled up on the makeshift bed Annie had made for her in the corner. She felt sorry for her cousin but somewhere inside her she felt shame too. Shame that she was related to her and that the gossiping that would surely follow would somehow stick to her too.

Her head filled with Charlie Mathieson's image. What would he think if he knew that her cousin was, well, unwed and going to have a bairn? She crept from the room and into the kitchen where her mother was stirring porridge on the stove.

Annie eyed her daughter, looking for signs that she was accepting the situation with Nancy. "Did you sleep alright?" she asked cordially.

Lexie took the bowl of porridge and sat at the kitchen table. "What's going to happen to her?" she asked, her young eyes willing Annie to tell her everything would be alright.

Annie poured herself some tea and sat beside Lexie.

"The man who did this to her isn't going to marry her Lexie, so to answer your question, I just don't know. I'm going to see Isobella Anderson today, let her know what's happened and ask if the Salvation Army can do anything to help."

"And if they can't?" Lexie asked.

Annie's eyes stared at the tea, steaming in her cup. "I don't have any answer to that either Lexie, but one thing's for certain, she won't be put out on the streets to face this alone."

Lexie pushed the porridge away from her, nothing felt normal any longer and the joy she had felt when Charlie Mathieson had winked at her as he got off the tram, had been replaced by the realisation that she too, by association, now had something shameful to hide.

"I'll better be off to work then," she said flatly, "make sure at least one of us gets on."

Annie flinched at the remark. Lexie was taking this badly and the longer Nancy stayed with them, the worse things were going to get.

The walk to Baxters Offices helped calm Lexie's mind, but when Amy Fyffe asked her to come into her small room Lexie felt sure she was in trouble. Maybe Mrs Fyffe knew about Nancy, maybe the whole of Baxters was gossiping about her, behind her back.

The smile on Mrs Fyffe's face faded at the sight of Lexie's tight-lipped expression.

"Are you alright Lexie?" she asked. "Is something wrong?"

"I don't know, Mrs Fyffe," Lexie managed to say, "is it something I've done?"

Amy Fyffe eyed her young charge. "You've done nothing wrong Lexie, in fact, I'm so pleased with your progress that I've arranged for Baxters to pay for you to go to night school and learn how to use a typewriter."

Despite her self-inflicted shame, Lexie's eyes widened in disbelief. "Me," she mouthed, "learn to type on a real typewriter?"

Amy Fyffe's smile was back. "What do you think?"

Lexie nodded enthusiastically. Since Nancy's trouble, the appeal of being a weaver like her had faded and now, she was being offered a chance to make something of herself.

No one she knew could type, not even Sarah with all her education.

"And there's more," continued Mrs Fyffe, "Malvina Edwards in the Drawing Office is due to retire in a few months time and, well, if you come up to scratch with your typing, I intend recommending you for the post."

Lexie could hardly believe her ears. The nightmare of Nancy and her troubles faded into nothing as she contemplated becoming the typist in the Drawing Office and, better still, seeing Charlie Mathieson every day. "When do I start?" Lexie beamed.

"Tomorrow night, seven o'clock at Stobswell School. Ask for Miss Dow, she's the teacher, and I've something else for you," Amy Fyffe added conspiratorially opening her desk drawer and extracting a pair of white kid gloves, wrapped in cellophane.

She handed them over to Lexie. "Now that you're going to be a typist," she continued, pleased with Lexie's keenness, "you're going to need to look after those hands and fingers, so I want you to wear these gloves at all times when you're outside, especially in the winter."

Lexie drew them slowly from their wrapper. "They're beautiful," she breathed, "thank you Mrs Fyffe, thank you."

Amy Fyffe extended her hands in front of her, skin perfect and nails shining. "There," she said, "typist's hands."

To say that Lexie floated through the rest of the day was an understatement. Nancy's life may not be going well, but hers was, and with the selfishness of youth she dismissed her cousin's plight and concentrated on her wonderful self.

She would learn to type with the greatest of speed and when Malvina Edwards announced her retirement, Lexie would be waiting to proudly take over and Charlie Mathieson, well, he would find her irresistible. How could he not?

She stroked the kid gloves again. She would wear them always and have hands just like Mrs Fyffe, beautiful and skilful.

Euan had left for the police station and Ian had gone out to play football with his mates at the park. Lexie couldn't wait to tell Sarah all about her new typing classes and had left just after breakfast on the Saturday morning, so it was just Annie and Nancy in the house when there was a loud knocking at the door.

Nancy jumped up. "Do you think it's Billy back?" she asked, hope springing in her eyes.

"Let's see." Annie calmed her, moving towards the front door. "Let's hope so."

The figure of Billy filled the doorway, but it wasn't Billy Donnelly, it was Billy Dawson. His features were a mix of worry and anger as he removed his bonnet and held Annie's gaze.

"Please tell me you've heard from Nancy?" he asked tightly.

"She's here," replied Annie, "and she's fine."

Billy felt himself relax. "Can I see her?"

Annie moved aside allowing Billy to come into the hallway. "Before you go in," she whispered, "there's something you should know..."

"She's with child," Billy said, before Annie could say any more, "Charlie Cassiday's been to see me and told me all about Joe and a lad called Billy Donnelly."

Annie nodded. "You'd better come through then, she's in the kitchen and Billy, she's very fragile, so be careful."

The sight of Nancy at the kitchen table almost brought tears to Billy's eyes.

The beautiful young girl he knew was replaced by a shadow of despair and hopelessness.

"Nancy," he whispered, taking her hand and willing her to look at him.

"I know I haven't been the best father in the world to you," he began hoarsely, "but I'm here now and whatever happens I'll look after you." Billy wasn't sure how he was going to do this, nor how he was going to tell Josie about Nancy's plight, but right now in Annie's kitchen, he knew he wouldn't desert her.

Annie felt her heart beat faster in her chest as Billy's compassion for his troubled daughter overwhelmed her. Had he known about his own son, would he have felt the same way towards her plight? She pushed the thought from her head. That was the past, this was now and Nancy needed all the help she could get.

"Is the father going to marry you?" he asked gently.

Nancy shook her head. "He's sinned," she murmured, "and he'll never be forgiven by God." Her eyes met Billy's. "And, neither will I."

Billy looked at Annie. *What's all this Catholic nonsense about?* he thought. *Hadn't they fought a World War so that people could be free from oppression like this?*

"I need to find Joe, Nancy," Billy said. "Do you have any idea where he is?"

"Joe!" Billy could see the fear welling up in Nancy's eyes.

"It's alright," he assured her, "I just need to speak with him about things, that's all."

Nancy shook her head. "I think I want to go and lie down now Auntie Annie," she said softly, "I feel so sick."

Annie helped her to her feet and guided her though to Lexie's room. "Just rest now, Nancy, everything will be alright." She stroked the dark hair of her niece, her heart breaking at what she must be going through.

Billy was pacing the kitchen floor when she returned. Just as he had done when she first laid eyes on Billy Dawson, he filled the room with his presence.

"I have to find Joe," he stated, "he's gone crazy about Billy Donnelly and Nancy and when he finds out Nancy's pregnant I don't know how he'll react."

Annie clutched her neck, her mind racing. "Billy Donnelly lives in Lochee," she told him. "Euan knows exactly where, but I don't think Joe does."

"Is Euan on duty today?"

Annie nodded. "Then I'll head down to Bell Street. Between the both of us, we can hopefully head off a killing."

Annie gasped. "Surely not, Billy, Joe's not a killer."

"He's not in control of himself anymore Annie," Billy told her. "I don't know what he'll do if he comes across the man, but it won't be pleasant."

For a moment, Billy wanted to take Annie in his arms and just hold her, but instead he headed for the door.

"Don't open it for anyone you don't know and certainly not Joe."

Annie nodded. She too, had wanted the strength of Billy's arms around her, but she had Euan and he would support her, she knew, guilt at her thoughts colouring her face.

Lexie bounced back home an hour later, but the mood of gloom quickly deflated her bubble. She looked around her. "Where's Nancy?" she asked.

"Sleeping, I hope," sighed Annie.

Lexie put her arm around her mother's shoulders, with such tenderness that Annie burst into tears.

"Lexie, Lexie," she gulped, "please don't let anything like this happen to you."

Lexie coloured, the memory of Robbie Robertson flooding her mind again. How she hated him and how he'd made her still feel tarnished from his touch.

"Never," Lexie insisted to Annie, with more confidence than she felt. "I'm a good girl and I'm going to be a typist," she beamed, showing her mother the cellophane package that held the kid gloves.

The statement was so ludicrous that Annie laughed through her tears. Lexie was such an innocent, she told herself, of course life for her would be better. Not for her daughter the shame of illegitimacy and loss, no, Lexie would have a wonderful life as a typist, in an office, with white kid gloves to wear. She thanked Billy Dawson silently, knowing it was his doing that had brought about the change in circumstances for her daughter and now, hopefully, he could do the same for Nancy.

The beat constables had been on the lookout for Joe Cassiday all day, but with no luck and Billy Dawson's suggestion that he and Euan needed to find Billy Donnelly and warn him was welcome news to his ears.

No one knew better than him, the history between Annie and Billy, but the life he had formed with Annie, gave him assurance that Billy no longer had a place in her heart.

"Let's find him then Mr Dawson, before anything nasty happens," Euan agreed, remembering how Alex Melville had put Billy in his place regarding Annie, so very long ago now. Yes, lots of water had flowed under many bridges, but in a small town like Dundee, no one was ever totally free of their past.

The two men headed for Lochee, their joint desire to protect Nancy spurring them on.

Billy Donnelly had been a disappointment to Euan when it came to standing up to his responsibility, but he didn't deserve to be murdered for his immaturity.

"He lives up here." Euan pointed to the close of a tall tenement of houses. "Two stairs up on the left."

Billy nodded. "Let's go," he said, the calmness that came with action descending upon him.

It took a few minutes before the door opened a crack and Billy Donnelly's eyes peered into the gloom of the stairwell.

Billy heard the sharp intake of breath when the lad saw Euan MacPherson.

"Can we come in Billy?"

The door opened further and Billy and Euan entered, Euan in the lead.

Billy's mother and father sat either side of the fireplace, the distress of the situation weighing heavily on their shoulders.

"I take it you know why we're here?" he asked Billy.

"I know, it's about Nancy," he murmured, shaking his head steadily all the time he spoke.

"Not quite," said Euan. "It's more about Joe Cassiday."

The fear that swept over the young man was almost visible.

"He knows!" Billy whispered, burying his head in his hands. "He'll kill me."

"Not if we can help it," Euan continued. He pointed to Billy Dawson. "This is Nancy's real father," he said, "and he knows Joe Cassiday from way back."

Billy Donnelly looked shocked. "So, if you're Nancy's real father, what's Joe Cassiday to Nancy?"

"Her stepfather," Billy said bluntly. "Have you any idea where he might be?"

"Stepfather," Billy mouthed, his eyes widening, "so that was it."

"That was what?" asked Euan.

Billy seemed to get strength from somewhere, his voice more normal when he spoke again.

"That was why he hated me," he continued, understanding beginning to filter into his mind. "He wanted her for himself!"

Euan and Billy exchanged looks. This was all getting very messy.

Euan cleared his throat. "So, if you hear from him Billy, or spot him anywhere, stay clear lad, he's out to get you."

Billy's mother muffled a scream. "It's alright Ma," he said, suddenly understanding everything. "It's not God who needs to forgive me and Nancy, it's us who need to forgive Joe Cassiday."

The lad seemed to grow in stature before their eyes. Somehow, he had found a way out of the guilt that had consumed him. He had felt he deserved to be punished, but now, he felt it was Joe Cassiday who was the true sinner.

He extended his hand to Euan and Billy. "Thanks," he said, "for the warning and Mr Dawson," he continued, "tell Nancy, I'll be back to see her soon."

The two men went out into the street and began walking back to Bell Street.

"I don't know what happened there," Euan said, "but I think someone just became a man today."

Billy nodded in agreement. "Let's hope so," he said, "for Nancy's sake."

"Now we've just to find Joe before he goes totally off his head," Euan acknowledged sagely. "Let's hope we're not too late."

Chapter 23

It was with the lightness of a guilt-free heart that Billy Donnelly knocked on Father Monaghan's door. The priest had just finished his lunch followed by a drop or two of Communion wine and was in a fine frame of mind.

"Why, it's young Mr Donnelly," he said, extending a hand in welcome. "Come away in and sit yourself down. Billy looked around the Spartan surroundings and chose an upright chair beside a small gate-leg table. It was cold and dreary in the room, but the priest more than made up for it with the brightness of his smile.

"And what brings you here, Billy?" he asked, settling himself at the other side of the table. He'd known Billy since birth and his Catholic upbringing had served to keep him on the 'straight and narrow' but he'd been worried about him of late. He had developed into a man with all the temptations that brought, and at his last confession had admitted there was a young woman who had smitten him with her looks and wiles, and it had taken quite a few Hail Mary's to earn forgiveness from the Catholic church.

Billy cleared his throat and got straight to the point. "I'm here to ask if you'll marry Nancy and me... and as soon as possible."

Father Monaghan blinked in astonishment. Surely the two of them had hardly met and now he wanted to marry her! But, even as he thought it, he realised there could be only one reason for the haste.

"Before we speak of marriage Billy, is there anything else you'd like to tell me?"

Billy felt the colour rush to his cheeks but held his nerve.

"She… we… are going to be having a bairn."

There, it was said and he waited for the priest's response. Billy knew the rules, not until marriage should you touch a woman *that way*, for it was surely a sin and to compound the sin, the result was a baby, out of wedlock. A bastard, they called it.

Any warmth the priest had from the wine, drained from his soul. He had met this situation before and hadn't found the way forward then and had no doubt that he wouldn't find it this time either.

"Is she a Catholic girl?" he asked.

Billy shook his head. "No, Father."

The priest inhaled deeply.

"Will she be willing to change her religion do you think?" Again Billy shook his head.

"Then you must know that the church can't recognise your marriage to this girl, Billy, let alone have me conduct the ceremony."

Billy's shoulders slumped. All the years he'd gone to Mass, done his bit, kept his side of the bargain with Father Monaghan and now, when he needed his Catholic faith the most, it wasn't there.

"So, what's to be done, Father?" he asked, already knowing the answer.

Father Monaghan sighed, as much in hopelessness at the situation as his inability to give Billy the answer that he wanted. The church was firm on the sanctity of marriage and unless Billy gave up this girl, there was only one way for him to go.

"Excommunication," the priest said solemnly, "and may God forgive you."

Billy pulled himself up to his full height. "If it's a sin to love a woman and to want her so badly that you'd die for her, then I'm guilty as charged, and if the Catholic Church doesn't like it, I want no more to do with it." Disillusioned, and before the priest could say another word, he turned on his heel and headed out into the world and Nancy, vowing never to leave her again and never to cross the threshold of a chapel again either. Annie had been pacing the floor for the last hour willing Euan to return with some good news. Nancy had been sick again and the pregnancy was leaving her listless and drained.

"Euan will be home soon," she said gently, "and things will get better." She led Nancy through to her bed again just as there was a knock at the door.

Hurrying to answer it, Annie knew it wouldn't be Euan but was fearful that Joe Cassiday might be on the other side. She called out, "Who is it?"

"Isobella!" came the startled reply. Annie threw open the door and the figure of her sister-in-law filled the doorway.

"Isobella, how wonderful to see you, come in, come in. Here, let me take your coat."

A bemused Isobella let Annie fuss around her.

"It's only me," she said, "not the Queen of Sheba. What's going on?"

"You must be a mind reader," Annie began, "turning up like this, just when I needed you most." She ushered her sister-in-law into the kitchen, "you're the only one I can trust with what I'm about to tell you and I hope you'll be able to help."

Isobella was the wife of a Salvation Army captain, John Anderson, and Alex Melville's sister, and it was she who had rescued Annie from her brother's violent temper.

"If I can, Annie," she said, "but not before I've had a cup of tea and a slice of your delicious fruitcake." Annie hurriedly put the kettle on and brought down the cake tin from the dresser shelf.

Isobella watched all of this activity with amusement, until she realised that Annie was acting on her nerves rather than her normal energy and when, at last, Annie sat down and poured out the tea, Isobella gently squeezed her arm.

"Whatever it is Annie," she said, "it will sort."

Annie tried to smile at her kindness. "I don't know if it will," she said, "not this time."

Isobella waited till Annie was ready to talk, and once she began to relate the sorry tale the words poured out.

"And, Nancy," asked Isobella, "she's here with you now?"

"She's Mary's daughter Isobella," she whispered, her voice cracking with emotion. "I can't see her on the streets, but I just don't know where to turn."

Sixteen years ago, Isobella's husband had left her and ran away to Edinburgh with Mary, leaving Annie to look after Nancy. But, thanks to Alex Melville's intervention, both John Anderson and Mary had come back to Dundee, Mary to be reunited with her child and John to return home to his wife. And now this had happened, Mary's daughter pregnant and unmarried.

Annie wouldn't have blamed Isobella for turning her back on the situation, but her Christian spirit was strong and the depth of her forgiveness immeasurable.

"There is a way forward," she assured Annie, "and if Nancy is agreeable, I can arrange a place for her where she can wait out her confinement. It's a nursing home on the outskirts of the town called Clement Park. There will be other young girls there, in the same condition as Nancy, but when the baby is born, decisions may have to be taken quickly for its welfare."

Annie felt tears build up in her eyes. Nothing had changed in the eighteen years since she had given birth to Billy Dawson's son in the poorhouse in Belfast and another generation of women were left to face life with or without their child, but with no husband. At least Clement Park wasn't the workhouse and with Isobella looking after things, Annie felt Nancy and her unborn baby would be safe there.

"Thank you Isobella," said Annie, holding her sister-in-law's hand tightly, "I won't forget this and neither will Mary watching over Nancy from heaven."

The sound of heavy footsteps signalled the return of Euan with Billy Dawson.

Annie rushed to the door. "Is it good news?" she asked breathlessly. "Have you found Joe yet? Please tell me Billy Donnelly is alright."

"Hush Annie," said Euan. "Questions, questions, questions." He looked at Billy Dawson. "Do you want to tell Nancy the good news?"

Billy nodded.

"Good news!" Annie exclaimed.

"We think the young man's had a change of heart and there'll be a marriage after all."

Annie clasped her hands in joy before throwing her arms around Billy.

The sudden closeness of her impulsive hug took both of them by surprise, but it was Billy who untangled himself from her first as Euan watched the encounter.

As Billy disappeared into the bedroom to tell Nancy some good news at last, Annie remembered Isobella was still in the kitchen.

"Isobella's here," she said to Euan, overly bright, aware that he was watching her carefully. "She's just offered to help Nancy, but if it's true that Billy Donnelly is going to marry her, then it won't now be necessary, will it...?" Her voice tailed off as she realised how almost hysterical she sounded. Was it just the good news that had made her throw herself at Billy Dawson, or some deep impulse from long ago that hadn't quite died?

Euan had picked up on her behaviour, but had Billy Dawson?

She tried to calm herself down by refilling the kettle and rinsing the teacups out under the tap, while Isobella stood up to go.

"Well, I'm glad that this young man is going to do the right thing," she said, "but if anything changes Annie, let me know and I'll make the arrangements."

Annie was calm again. "Thanks Isobella," she said softly now, "hopefully the arrangements we'll be making will be for a wedding."

Billy left without saying goodbye and Nancy emerged from the bedroom; for the first time, a hint of colour was on her cheeks.

"He said Billy's coming to see me soon." She threw her arms around Annie's neck, animation coming back into her small frame and life returning to her eyes. "Thank you Auntie Annie for everything and as soon as Billy comes for me, I'll be going to be with him in Lochee."

Annie beamed. "That's wonderful Nancy," she said, "but there's no need to rush now, you're carrying a child and that's the most important thing to remember."

Relief was now flooding through Annie. Nancy would be a respectable married woman soon and if the babe was born a little early, then who's to notice?

Lexie took the news with the casualness of youth. "So does that mean I'll get my room back soon?"

Annie looked at her daughter, not yet a woman, nor touched by the hand of fate with all its vagaries in developing compassion and understanding for the human condition. She put her arms around her daughter. "Yes, Lexie, you can have your room back soon and thank you for all your kindness."

It was a week after Billy Donnelly and Nancy wed at Dundee Registrar's Office, with her father at her side and Annie as Matron of Honour, that the news reached Annie that Joe Cassiday had been found collapsed on the Law Hill and was now in a bad way in Dundee Royal Infirmary.

One of Euan's constables had found him almost frozen to death and starving, and the fear was that he had deliberately chosen to end his life.

"What about Agnes?" Annie asked Euan. "Does she know this?"

Euan nodded. "She's been at his bedside since he was brought in, her and their three little boys. Despite everything, she still seems to love the man and blames Nancy for everything."

Annie was shocked. "But, surely it was Joe who was at fault, lusting after

Nancy like a dog in heat."

Euan winced at Annie's bluntness. "Maybe so," he said, "but she says Nancy encouraged it."

Much as she didn't want to believe it of her niece, she remembered Mary and her flirtatious ways with Billy Dawson when he first came to their small farm to help with the flax harvest. Maybe it had come through in the blood and Nancy was as much to blame as Joe Cassiday. She pushed the thought from her head. Nancy was now a respectable married woman and that was all that mattered.

"Does Billy Dawson know?" she asked Euan.

"He does," came the reply, "and he's going to the DRI to visit him this evening, see how things are and maybe get him back to some kind of life with Agnes."

To say Billy was shocked when he saw Joe was a huge understatement. He remembered him in his Black Watch kilt striding off to war, full of life and strong as an ox. It was hard to believe this was the same man. Agnes was sitting by Joe's side 'to be there when he wakens', she'd said, but by the looks of the colour of Joe's skin, that wasn't going to be any time soon.

"Maybe you should go home Agnes," Billy said, "look after your laddies and get some rest. I'll sit with him for a while."

Reluctantly, Agnes rose. "You're a good man, Billy Dawson," she said, "but if you see that daughter of yours, tell her from me, I'll never forgive her for the harm she's done to Joe... never." Billy was taken aback by the vehemence of her words. What was Agnes trying to imply? Surely, Nancy would never have encouraged such attention?

Billy lowered himself into the chair Agnes had vacated and looked around him. The ward was quiet at this time of the evening, apart from a few moans and coughs from the other patients and the nurses going about their duties.

"How's he been?" Billy asked one of them as she passed Joe's bed.

The woman shook her head. "It's in the hands of the Lord, now," she said softly, "if he's lucky, he'll just sleep away."

Billy took Joe's ice cold hand in his. "Good God, man, how did you end up like this?" he murmured, his mind going back to his first encounter with the handsome Irishman at Baxters Mill where Joe was a tenter and all the women fancied him, including Annie.

Is this what love does to you? he wondered. *Love so strong that all common sense flies out of the window.* His thoughts turned to Annie again and to Mary who came to him pregnant with his child and whom he'd married. What would life have been like if he and Annie...? He shook his head, not wishing to think of what might have been.

He had Josie now and three beautiful daughters, and Annie, well, she had Euan and Ian and Lexie from her marriage to Alex Melville. Yes, too much water under the bridge, and now there was no going back.

Without warning, Joe eyes suddenly opened. "MARY," he cried, "IS IT YOU?"

A wide grin lit up his gaunt face and a light filled his eyes. "I'm coming," he whispered. "Wait for me." Then as quickly as it came, the smile faded and the light left Joe's eyes. Billy tightened his grip on his hand as the nurse hurried over to her patient. She lifted his eyelid and felt for his pulse.

"He's gone," she said softly, releasing Billy's grip from Joe's hand. "He's at peace now."

"I hope so," Billy murmured, stunned at the speed of Joe's passing. "He's gone to be with Mary again," he added hoarsely, searching for understanding in the nurse's eyes. "She came for him."

The nurse looked at him kindly. "Perhaps you should go home now Mr Dawson, there's no more you can do for him, we'll deal with things now."

Billy's footsteps again led to Annie's door. Euan answered his knock.

"It's Joe," he said, "he died tonight." A despairing look came into his eyes. "And all for love," he added, sadly. "All for love."

Billy shook his head. "Take care of Annie," he said, "she loved Joe once, but I ruined it for her and now, it's all too late."

Without another word, Billy started back down the stairs, turning left into Albert Street and Princes Street before finally climbing the steepness of Dens Brae. The hospital would have sent word of Joe's death to Agnes as his next of kin, but Charlie would still be unaware that his brother had passed.

A flicker of light showed through the weave of the curtains covering the small kitchen window and knowing what news he would be bringing, Billy hesitated before knocking gently on the window pane. Within seconds the curtains parted and the white face of Charlie Cassiday froze before him.

The door was unlocked and Billy let himself into the hovel.

"He's gone, isn't he?" muttered Charlie, hardly able to speak the words.

Billy's eyes couldn't hold the pain he saw before him. "I was with him," Billy said, trying to soften the blow, "so he didn't die alone."

"Does Agnes know?" Charlie asked, his rheumy eyes brimming with tears.

"I think the hospital will have told her, Charlie, but if you like I'll make sure..."

Charlie shook his head. "She's a good woman, Billy, and neither Joe, nor that daughter of yours, should have treated her so badly, so I'll see to her needs, not you."

Billy flinched. Did Charlie really believe that Joe was an innocent in all this? But, now wasn't the time for recriminations, the man needed help.

"I'll call round tomorrow Charlie, do what I can to make sure Joe gets a decent burial."

To take help from Billy Dawson stuck in Charlie's throat, but poverty decided the issue.

"Thank you," he said, his voice steadying. "He didn't deserve a pauper's grave."

True to his word, Billy paid for everything. The Mass was held at St Patrick's with just Charlie, Agnes and the three boys, Billy and Josie, and Annie and Euan attending.

Agnes wouldn't allow Nancy anywhere near, but as the hearse turned into the Eastern Cemetery, Billy could see his daughter and Billy Donnelly amongst the crowd that had gathered at the cemetery gates.

Billy and Annie recognised old workers from Baxters who had known Joe when he worked there as a tenter. Dockers from the harbour, their hooks hanging from their belts, flanked the crowd, and men from Joe's old regiment, the Black Watch, stood ramrod straight, bonnets in hand as the coffin passed. But Agnes only had eyes for Nancy.

She had been nursing her anger for months now, long before Joe had passed away, and the sight of her hanging onto the arm of Billy Donnelly was the last straw.

Charlie could see the look in her eye and knew her mind was not steady. "Not here," he whispered to her, "not at Joe's funeral."

But Agnes leapt out of the hearse. "If not here," she spat, "then where?"

With a speed that belied her years, Agnes crossed the gravel path towards Nancy. The crowd parted for her, not understanding what was happening but knowing she was unstoppable and in a split second, the knife she had hidden in her shawl, flashed before Nancy's eyes.

"It should be YOU being buried," she screamed, "NOT JOE!" as she tried to plunge the knife into Nancy's chest. Instinctively, Nancy drew back as Billy Donnelly reached across her to protect her from the blow. The knife slashed into his arm before two of the men grabbed Agnes and wrenched the knife from her bloody hand.

For a minute everyone froze before Euan took charge. He blew his police whistle to summon any beat policemen who would be near and pulled a scarf from Annie's neck and started to apply a tourniquet to try to staunch the flow of blood. Billy Dawson held a trembling Nancy in his arms as the sound of running boots came closer.

Two of Euan's constables took over the first aid while Euan knelt down beside the collapsed Agnes. "Can you see to it that Billy and Nancy get to Maryfield Hospital in that car of yours?" he asked Billy. "And, stay with them till I get there."

Billy nodded and looked at Charlie. "Will you be alright to look after things here Charlie, for Joe's sake?"

On hearing this, the priest who was holding Charlie's arm began to guide him back to the graveside. "Your brother needs you now, more than ever," he whispered, "so let's see him safely into the ground."

Annie and Josie took Agnes's three boys back to Annie's home. They were both in such a state of shock, no one spoke a word and Annie prayed that Nancy's unborn child would be kept safe in her womb, protected by nature.

Josie took control of the kettle and made sweet tea for everyone, and using her skills as a teacher, settled the three young boys down, before quietly taking her leave of Annie and the situation.

"I'm sorry this has happened to your family," she acknowledged sincerely at the door. "I'm sure Mr MacPherson will be back as soon as possible, but if there's anything..."

Annie waved the offer away. "No... Thank you Josie," she said. "You've done more than enough already. Your own daughters will be wondering where you are."

Their eyes met and both of them felt a stir of jealousy for the other.

Over the years Josie had believed that Billy's past was just that and the people in it were no more than mere shadows, but today she realised just how real these shadows actually were to her husband and how, no matter how she tried to deny it, they could still destroy the life she had built up with Billy Dawson.

Chapter 24

Within an hour of their arrival at Maryfield Hospital, Billy's wound had been stitched and the doctor was confident that there was no nerve damage. He was sleeping off the chloroform, but would be fine to go home in about an hour or so.

On hearing the news, Nancy eventually stopped trembling and some colour returned to her cheeks.

"Are you feeling better, Nancy?" Billy Dawson asked, unsure how deeply to dig into the incident at the cemetery.

"She was right, you know," Nancy said without prompting, "about me."

"Right?" echoed Billy. Nancy nodded.

"I did 'egg him on' at times," she admitted, "just to annoy Agnes, you see. But it didn't mean anything," she stressed, "it was just supposed to be funny."

Billy wasn't sure how to answer her, obviously Agnes hadn't seen the funny side of Nancy's behaviour, nor did Billy.

Perhaps his daughter was more like her mother than he had realised. Mary had flirted with him outrageously that night at the farm, stirring him up till he could hold back no longer. He'd taken her that night and regretted it bitterly the next day. Annie would never have forgiven him for his weakness, so he had left before anymore could happen. He knew that her feelings for him were love and not lust, but when Mary had followed him to Scotland, pregnant with his child, he felt that fate had dealt him the cards he deserved.

"What'll happen to her?" Nancy asked, guilt sitting heavily on her shoulders.

Before he could answer her, Euan MacPherson's uniformed presence came into the waiting room.

Nancy spoke first. "How is she Sergeant MacPherson? Agnes I mean."

"Not good," said Euan, "she's been remanded in custody till the Procurator Fiscal deals with it on Monday and now that the fight's gone out of her, well, she's just a poor soul, Nancy."

"She won't go to jail, will she?" Nancy asked, tension creeping back into her muscles.

Euan MacPherson took a deep breath and sat down on one of the chipped wooden chairs, motioning Billy to include himself into the conversation.

"It's like this Nancy," he began, "at worst, what Agnes tried to do was deliberate, what the law calls premeditated. In other words, she planned to kill you and if it hadn't been for your husband's intervention, she may very well have succeeded. There were plenty of witnesses to her act, so she would be looking at an attempted murder charge and, if found guilty, a long prison sentence.

"At best, she could be charged with grievous bodily harm, if Mr Donnelly decides to press charges and again, with the amount of people who saw what happened, she would be found guilty and face at least five years in prison."

Nancy's face paled again. "But she didn't mean it, I know she didn't," she blurted out hysteria whipping through the words. "It was me who caused all this trouble, I knew Joe liked me and I took to showing off in front of her, making out I liked him too... but," the words tapered off. "I didn't mean any of it... please believe me."

Beseeching eyes turned from Euan MacPherson to Billy Dawson and back again.

Billy could hardly believe his ears as he heard his daughter's confession and now a good man had died for the love of her and a good woman was in a jail cell awaiting her punishment.

"What's to be done, Euan?" Billy asked, drawing him aside and out of earshot from the tearful Nancy. "Well, Billy, that's up to Nancy and, of course, Billy Donnelly. Judging by what she's just said, I doubt if she'll take things any further and unless Mr Donnelly wants some kind of revenge against Joe Cassiday by condemning Agnes to a life in prison, well..."

The door through to the treatment room opened, and Billy came through, his arm in a sling and a small bottle of pills in his hand.

Nancy rushed towards him. "Billy, Billy!" she wailed. "Agnes is in jail and it's all my fault."

Billy winced as she crushed herself against his arm. "Hold back Nancy," he said through gritted teeth, pushing her gently away.

Euan MacPherson and Billy walked over to the pair. "How are you son?" Euan asked.

Billy nodded. "I'll be fine," he said, "but no thanks to that mad woman."

Nancy intervened again. "We need to talk about Agnes," she insisted, "before it's too late."

Billy looked confused. "Before what's too late?" he asked.

Nancy looked at Euan. "Will you tell him please Sergeant MacPherson?" she begged, before turning her tearful eyes on Billy Donnelly. "I'll wait outside for your answer," she added, casting a longing glance at her husband as she left. "Please be kind," she said. "I love you."

There was no easy way to tell the young man that his new wife had a 'flirtatious nature' to say the least, so Euan MacPherson couched it in terms of 'youthful indiscretion' and 'misunderstanding' that had caused Agnes to react the way she had. Billy knew all about misunderstandings, didn't his father almost end up in jail because of a 'misunderstanding' with the bookie at Polepark.

"So," he surmised, "there's no chance that she'll try anything like this again?"

"I think she'll have enough on her plate with these three laddies to look after," said Euan, "and if I'm right, Charlie Cassiday will be around to keep an eye on things."

Billy Dawson held his breath.

"Whatever you say, Sergeant MacPherson," Billy said, finally, "I know you're a good man who knows what's right and wrong in this world."

The three men shook hands. "Now, go and find your wife and take her home, it's been a long day and we're all exhausted."

"Hold on," called Billy Dawson, hurrying after him, "I'll take you both home in the motor. Neither of you are in a fit state to walk any distance."

Euan waved them away. He was heading back to Bell Street to tell Agnes that she was free to go and that Charlie would help her with the bairns and getting back on her feet. Sometimes things just work out, he thought to himself, as he called the station for the Black Maria to come pick him up. Yes, sometimes, he decided, justice prevailed.

Now that Nancy was happily ensconced with Billy and the pregnancy was progressing without any problems from the drama at Joe's funeral, Annie felt the time was overdue for writing to Bella in Belfast. She'd want to know about Nancy and the baby and, of course, the marriage to Billy Donnelly and how well Lexie was getting on at Baxters Office. For the first time in a long time, Annie felt at peace. Ian was doing well at primary school and would be moving on to the 'big school' in the new year and all this she felt was down to Euan's loving care and calm strength. She smiled at the thought of her husband, not handsome like Joe Cassiday had been, not cruel like Alex Melville and been, and not intense like Billy Dawson. Just steady and reliable and always there when she needed him. She picked up her pen and wrote down all the news, signing her name with love and hoping to hear from Bella very soon, maybe even arrange a visit to Dundee. Surely, Dr Adams would let her have some time off.

She slipped on her coat and hurried out to post the letter. Her family would be home soon and she had the tea to get ready. Euan's favourite, mince and doughboys.

Ian was the first home, only staying long enough to change into his football boots before rushing out again.

"Tea's at six," she called after him. "Don't be late."

The mince and doughboys were cooking nicely and Annie was peeling the vegetables when Lexie breezed in. She had watched the changes in her daughter, particularly since she began her typing course and was proudly wearing her kid gloves every time she left the house. She would always be grateful to Billy Dawson for his help with Lexie. It was a pity that she and Billy's daughter Sarah now saw less and less of one another, but times had moved on and Sarah was preparing to go to university, an English degree, Lexie said, but added that Sarah may be going to be a teacher but she couldn't type. Had there been rivalry between the two girls? Annie hadn't noticed, but if there had, it didn't seem to be there any longer and even Josie, who had never been keen on Lexie, seemed to accept that their respective daughters would always remain friends.

"I can now type at twenty-five words per minute," she told Annie, grinning smugly. "Miss Dow timed me." She had certainly blossomed under Amy Fyffe's wing, but both women were unaware that the occasional visit to the Drawing Office to help Malvina Edwards cope with the filing, was another reason for the confidence she was now exuding.

Charlie Mathieson continued to flirt with her at every opportunity and one day, Lexie felt sure, he was going to ask her to go out with him. She wondered, in fact, in her naivety, how he'd managed to resist her for so long. It must be all of three months since she'd been working at Baxters Office and when you'd just turned sixteen years of age, three months seemed a very long time. After all, it had only taken Robbie Robertson two weeks to 'pop the question' but, of course, she had been too young to understand the ways of the world then, not like now.

Her young mind had also managed to erase Robbie's forced attention on her and as far as she was concerned, he no longer featured in her life. But, unfortunately, for Lexie, Robbie had not forgotten her, especially her rejection of his love and the humiliation of Sergeant MacPherson returning his ring to him.

Every day, from the dimness of Harry Duncan's Butchers Shop, he'd watch Lexie going into Baxters Offices, which were just across King Street from the shop and then watch her leave again, sometimes on her own, but sometimes with a tall, posh boy, who he found out worked in the Drawing Office.

Robbie didn't know what happened in a Drawing Office, but he did know that jealously stirred in his heart at the sight of the two of them walking towards the tram stop, him smoking a cigarette and her with her silly white gloves on.

It should have been him walking out with Lexie, not that 'lanky Tam', he decided. His mind raced in all directions trying to find a way to get close to Lexie again, make her understand that he was a real man and he still had the silver ring for her to wear again.

Just then, the 'enemy' came into view. There was no way he was going to let him get to Lexie first, and his mind formed the perfect solution as he watched Charlie Mathieson go past.

He hurried through to the back shop and tore a page from the order book.

Dear Lexie

Meet me Saturday nite under the clock in Reform Street at 7 and I take you to the picturs. You no who. Xxx

He folded the paper over twice and wrote 'LEXIE' on the front before crossing the road and pushing through the glass doors into the entrance way. There was only the cleaner, Maggie Rennie, mopping the floor and

Robbie beckoned her over.

"I need to leave this note for my girlfriend," he whispered, "she works in the office."

The cleaner took the note and squinted at the word. "Whit's her name?" she queried.

"Lexie," Robbie said, "Lexie Melville."

Typical of her life of poverty, she asked, "And whit's in it fir me?"

Robbie hadn't expected this. "What about a pork chop from Harry Duncan's next time you're in?"

The cleaner's eyes widened. "Yir on, son," she gurgled, pushing the note into her apron pocket.

Robbie relaxed. "You won't forget now, will you?" he said as the sound of heavy footsteps sounded in the stairwell. His heart was pounding as he ran out the door and across the street back to the safety of the butcher's shop.

Harry Duncan eyed him as he rushed past. "Somethin' on fire?" he asked.

"No, nothin' Mr Duncan, just forgot to get a message for Mum."

Harry Duncan shook his head. "The young nowadays," he muttered to himself. "Half daft."

The next morning when Lexie turned up for work, the note was on her desk.

Puzzled, she read the words and her heart leapt. Surely, it was a note from Charlie, he was too shy to ask her out face to face, so he'd left her the note.

She gazed at it again, surprised at the poor spelling, but not caring. Charlie Mathieson wanted to take her out to the pictures and she couldn't wait till Saturday.

Chapter 25

Early on Saturday morning, Lexie rushed over to Sarah's. A bleary-eyed Josie opened the door. "Lexie!" she whispered. "It's only eight o'clock, Sarah's still in bed..."

Lexie's eyes were shining with uncontrolled joy and Josie realised that the only thing that could be making her sparkle at eight in the morning was a BOY.

There was a time when this would have unnerved Josie completely, but Sarah was now firmly on track to become a teacher and nothing Lexie could say or do would change that.

"Well, I suppose..." She reluctantly let the excited girl in. Lexie ran up the hallway to Sarah's room and knocked urgently on the door.

"Open up, Sarah," she whispered loudly, "it's me, Lexie."

"Come in, the door's unlocked," answered Sarah, yawning her head off. "What's up?"

Lexie bounced in, a mile-wide grin on her face. She handed Sarah the note.

"Read that," she gushed, hugging herself with excitement.

Sarah propped herself up on her elbow and read the words. "It's not very well written," she observed, her grasp of English and grammar well above average, "and who is it from?"

Lexie ignored the comment about grammar. "It's from a junior draughtsman called Charlie Mathieson," she sighed. "He works at Baxters in the Drawing Office and oh Sarah, he's absolutely wonderful!"

"We've been flirting with one another for weeks now and I just knew he was going to ask me to go out with him, once he got over his shyness that is." She plucked the note back from Sarah's hand. "And now... this."

Lexie was obviously smitten, but Sarah had seen this before, with Robbie Robertson no less. "Is he the one then?" she asked, tongue in cheek. "I mean the man you really, really love this time."

The wind in Lexie's sails reduced down to a breeze. Sarah wasn't impressed, or maybe, she surmised, her friend was just a little bit jealous. Sarah had never been 'good with boys', in fact apart from the time she'd ran away from Davie Robertson in the park, to Lexie's knowledge, she'd never even spoken to another boy.

Poor Sarah, she thought. *Yes that's it, she's jealous.*

Lexie put her hand on Sarah's shoulder. "You still don't understand men, do you? Of course I don't know if he's the ONE yet, but he will be if I have anything to do with it. So, be happy for me Sarah and who knows, he may have a friend..."

Sarah pushed back the covers and dropped her legs over the edge of her bed, holding up her hands in mock fear.

"No, never," she cried, giggling. "Not another date in the park!"

Both girls collapsed in laughter onto Sarah's bed.

Just then, the bedroom door opened and Josie came in with a tray of tea and biscuits.

"What's all this noise?" she asked, smiling at the girl's exuberance. "Your dad's trying to sleep next door, not to mention your sisters."

"Sorry Mum," said Sarah, gulping back a giggle, "we'll keep it down."

The tea and biscuits tasted wonderful.

"So, what are you going to wear?" Sarah asked, suddenly lessening the smile on Lexie's face.

"Mmmmhhhh, there may be a problem there," she replied, "I don't have many things to choose from and I do want to look my very best."

Sarah immediately went to her wardrobe and produced a beautiful cream silk blouse with a huge floppy bow at the neck. Lexie's eyes widened. "Where did you get that?" she gasped. "It's beautiful."

"Mum bought it in Draffens' sale, she said I've to keep it for good, I think she meant for when I go to university, but you can borrow it, if you like."

Lexie couldn't believe her ears. "REALLY!"

Sarah smiled. "Of course, if you like it."

Lexie touched the soft fabric and marvelled at how the light caught it as she ran her fingers over the bow. "I like," she whispered. Saturday night was going to be wonderful.

With a final hug and the blouse safely in a brown paper bag Lexie skipped home.

She would wash her hair and pin kiss curls in the bobbed waves either side of her cheeks. Her stockings and garters were ready, and the new navy blue skirt she'd bought with her first two weeks' wages would look beautiful with the blouse.

Euan, Annie and Ian were having breakfast when she came in. Annie glanced at the clock – nine o'clock!

"Where have you been so early Lexie?" Annie asked, and judging by the rosiness of her daughter's cheeks she wondered for a moment if she'd slept at all.

Lexie pulled up a chair. "I've something to tell you," she said, after placing the paper bag carefully on the dresser.

Euan and Annie exchanged glances. They didn't like surprises where Lexie was concerned.

"Go on," said Annie.

Lexie cleared her throat. "You know I've been working at Baxters Office for three months now," she paused for confirmation.

Annie nodded. "And?"

"And," Lexie continued, "there's this junior draughtsman there, Charlie Mathieson, and, well," she felt herself begin to redden further, "he's asked me out to the pictures with him...TONIGHT!"

Ian broke the silence that suddenly filled the small kitchen. "What's a daftsman?" he asked.

Euan was the first to recover. "Never mind that now," he said gruffly, "if you've finished your porridge, go and tidy your room."

"But..."

"No buts," repeated Euan. "Your mother and me need to speak to Lexie."

Lexie felt herself go cold. They wouldn't stop her, would they? Nobody could be that cruel.

Euan handed his cup to Annie. "More tea dear," he said, "and a cup for Lexie."

He took his teacup and stood up. "I'll be in the other room," he told Annie, winking meaningfully. "I think it's time for you to have a chat with Lexie about... well, life!"

Annie got the message and flopped down on the kitchen chair next to her daughter. Euan was right, as usual, Lexie was growing up, and at sixteen needed to understand about 'men' especially junior draughtsmen, and it was up to Annie to explain things to her.

The next hour was, arguably, the worst hour of Lexie's young life as Annie tried to explain the pitfalls of falling in love. "Look at Nancy," she'd finally pointed out, "now you don't want that to happen to you!"

Lexie was suitably chastened. "We're just going to the pictures," she pouted, "and I'll be back home for ten o'clock."

Annie sighed. She couldn't stop her daughter growing up, but her own experiences had taught her that life didn't always work out as you wanted, especially when it came to love.

"Alright," she agreed, "but remember to be home by ten and if there's any trouble, your dad's constables will be on duty on Saturday night and he'll make sure they'll look out for you."

Lexie breathed a sigh of relief, although being told that the 'police' would be watching her, offended her grown-up status, she nodded in agreement.

"Thanks Mum," she said, "I'll be careful, trust me."

But even as she said it, Lexie was back in the park with Robbie Robertson, reliving the horror of that night. No, Annie had no need to worry she would be letting THAT happen again.

At half past six that evening, Lexie was ready. "What do you think?" she asked Annie, twirling round in front of her. "Will I do?"

Yes, her daughter was growing up and turning into a lovely young woman. Annie felt a small flutter of fear for her, as she reminded her of herself at that age, naive and trusting and, at that time, totally unaware of the ways of men.

"You'll do," said Annie. "Now remember, be back by ten and don't have me worrying about you."

She gave her mother a hug, and with a ladylike wave of her gloved hand swept out of the door.

Annie turned to Euan who'd been sitting quietly observing the floorshow. "Will she be alright Euan?" she asked, her forehead pulling into a worry line.

"She'll be fine," he assured her. "There are four constables on duty tonight in the town centre, two covering the Wellgate and Murraygate and two for the Nethergate and Overgate. If Lexie's meeting this lad at the clock, she'll be right in the middle of them all and they've been told to keep an eye out for her." He patted the space on the sofa next to him. "Come on, sit yourself down and get on with your knitting, she'll be fine."

The tram rattled to a stop at the City Square and Lexie stepped off, trying not to hurry across the road to the meeting place. After all, she didn't want to be the first to arrive, she should be the one to keep her suitor waiting, wasn't that how it worked?

Her eyes scanned the pavement, as she searched out the figure of Charlie Mathieson but in vain.

Crossing the road, she took up a position just to the side of the clock near where a newspaper seller was plying his trade. Glancing at the clock she saw it was five past seven. Charlie Mathieson was late.

By half past seven, Lexie could feel tears forming in her eyes and her chin begin to quiver when she heard a voice at her side.

"Waitin' for me?"

Lexie's heart leapt. He was here... at last, but the smile on her face faded instantly at the sight of Robbie Robertson grinning at her.

She could feel a surge of anger surface as embarrassment flooded her emotions.

"NO," she said loudly. "I'm not waiting for you, now GO AWAY."

But Robbie Robertson wasn't going anywhere.

"So, who are you waiting for Lexie?"

Lexie couldn't contain herself any longer, and bursting into tears, shoved Robbie backwards into the flow of pedestrians. "GET AWAY FROM ME," she screamed, her legs wobbling as she turned to make her humiliating escape up the Murraygate.

But the strong arms of Constable O'Rourke stopped her progress. He'd been watching the encounter from the top of Castle Street and could see that the meeting was not going as planned. "Hey up, lassie," he said, "what's the bother?"

Lexie looked over her shoulder at Robbie Robertson, apologising to two women for crashing into them and shrugging his shoulders in the direction of Lexie.

Of all the people to witness her humiliation, it had to be Robbie Robertson.

"I'm alright," she said through tears and sobs, "I just want to go home."

Constable O'Rourke guided her to the police box outside the bank and asked her to wait.

Once inside, he telephoned the station and asked for transport to come to the police box at once, by order of Sergeant Macpherson. "You'll be home soon," the policeman said kindly, wondering what on earth Sergeant MacPherson's daughter was doing with Harry Duncan's butcher boy.

It was only just past nine o'clock when Lexie was brought home. Her tear-stained face and distraught appearance told a different story from when Lexie had gone out to meet Charlie Mathieson.

Euan was on his feet instantly, his eyes locking on to PC O'Rourke who was standing by the door, while Annie wrapped her arms around her daughter.

"What happened Andy?" he asked the constable, eyeing Lexie with concern, "she's in a right state."

"She seemed to be waiting for the young man to turn up, but when Robbie Robertson did arrive, she didn't want..."

Euan held up his hand. "What's Robbie Robertson got to do with this?"

The constable looked confused. "Well, isn't that who she was waiting for?"

Euan's lips tightened. "Thanks Andy," he said, "for bringing her home, leave it with me now and I'll see you on Monday."

Annie had calmed Lexie down and the whole story unfolded. Charlie Mathieson hadn't turned up as agreed, but the horrible Robbie Robertson had come along, by chance, and saw her standing there on her own and guessed the rest. She'd been 'stood up'.

"He was laughing at me Mum," Lexie wailed. "I hate him, I just hate him."

Annie hushed her daughter, relieved that no real harm had been done, except perhaps to her pride, and sure that Lexie would get over this in a few days' time.

"I'm going to bed now," Lexie murmured, still sniffing, "and I'm never going to speak to Charlie Mathieson again... EVER."

By Monday morning, Lexie had some control back and determined that Charlie Mathieson wasn't worth hurting over. Maybe Sarah had been right all along, boys were nothing but trouble. She turned into Baxters Office, watched by Robbie Robertson as he filled the trays in the shop window with strings of sausages and mounds of mince. *Not so clever now are we Lexie Melville?* he smiled, sniggering to himself. How easy it had been to fool her into thinking that the 'drippy draughtsman' fancied her. "She'll be back," he said under his breath, "one day."

"What's that you're saying?" Harry Duncan asked.

"Nothin' Mr Duncan," Robbie answered, "nothin' at all."

Lexie began pounding the typewriter with venom, bringing herself to Amy Fyffe's attention.

"Lexie," she enquired, "what are you doing? It's trained fingers a typewriter needs not sledgehammers!"

Lexie stopped typing, her head hanging down and her eyes misting again at the memory of her humiliation.

Amy Fyffe waited.

"I'm sorry Mrs Fyffe," she muttered, "I'm not feeling too well."

Amy Fyffe immediately ushered her into her small office and sat her down. She could see Lexie wasn't her usual exuberant self but she didn't seem really ill.

"Do you want to tell me about it?" she asked gently.

The simple act of kindness was all it took for the tears to start again and Lexie poured out the sorry tale about the note and of Charlie Mathieson's non-appearance.

"Charlie Mathieson," Amy said, "from our Drawing Office?"

Lexie nodded.

Amy Fyffe was more than shocked. Charlie Mathieson was her nephew.

"Leave this with me," she told Lexie. "Now dry your eyes, have a cup of tea and concentrate on your typing. I'll be back soon." Charlie Mathieson, she thought, her sister's son, behaving in such a boorish way, surely not.

Amy hurried into the Drawing Office and straight to Malvina Edwards' desk. "I need to speak with Charlie," she said, "privately." Malvina nodded.

"Nothing bad, I hope," Malvina whispered in the silence of the Drawing Office.

She knew Charlie was Amy's nephew. "I'll send him out in a few minutes with some drawings for the engineers. Wait for him outside their office."

Malvina gathered together a bundle of blueprints and signalled Charlie to come to her desk. "Take these to the Engineers' Office, please Charlie," she instructed, "and right away."

"Immediately Miss Edwards," Charlie responded, gathering the prints and tucking them under his arm.

Amy Fyffe was waiting.

"Auntie Amy," Charlie smiled, "are you waiting for the engineers?"

"No Charlie," she replied curtly, "I'm waiting for you."

Charlie looked confused. "ME!" he exclaimed.

She drew him aside to the landing at the top of the stairwell. "It's about Lexie Melville,"

Charlie's eyes lit up at the mention of Lexie's name. "What about her?" he asked, "she's a real smasher isn't she."

"If she's a 'real smasher' as you put it Charlie, then why did you leave the poor girl standing in the street on Saturday night waiting for you to turn up to take her to the pictures?"

Charlie looked stunned. "Auntie Amy, I don't know what you're talking about. I never arranged to meet Lexie on Saturday, although I wish I did have the courage to ask her out."

It was Amy's turn to be confused. "So, you never sent her a note asking her to meet you?"

Charlie shook his head. "But what's this all about?" He frowned. "If I didn't send her the note, then who did?"

"That's for me to find out Charlie." She patted her nephew on the shoulder, "I think Miss Edwards will be wanting these blueprints back," she said, "they were just a way to have a word with you about all this. Lexie's very upset," she added, "she thinks you 'stood her up'."

"But, I would never..."

Amy waved her hand to stop him saying anything further. "I know that, and I'll make sure Lexie knows it too."

Chapter 26

When Lexie arrived home from work on Monday, her spirits seemed to be miraculously restored. "You seem much better," Annie said, glad that her daughter was more like herself.

"I am sooooooo much better," she replied, exaggerating the statement. "It wasn't Charlie who sent me the note and Mrs Fyffe has sorted it all out."

"Really?"

"Mmmmhhhhh, yes, he's her nephew you see and she just knew he wouldn't do a thing like that."

"Well that's good news," agreed Annie, "but if it wasn't Charlie Mathieson who left you the note, then who was it?"

"Don't know and don't care," she beamed, "'cause me and Charlie are going to the pictures FOR REAL next Saturday and he's going to pick me up here and not on some street corner... if that's alright Mum," she added quickly, remembering her manners.

Euan came home at six o'clock to find Annie and Lexie chattering away in the kitchen as they both busied themselves with the tea things, and was relieved to see that Lexie seemed to have recovered from her 'ordeal'.

"Someone's happy," he smiled, hanging up his tunic and helmet on the hallstand and embracing an excited Lexie as she ran to welcome him.

"You'll never guess what's happened..." she began.

"Now, Lexie," Annie chided her, "let your dad get in the door."

Euan looked at Annie for explanation.

"She's found out that it wasn't Charlie Mathieson who sent her the note and Mrs Fyffe, who just happens to be his auntie, has sorted things out. The upshot is Charlie is taking her to the pictures this Saturday and he's going to collect her here..." She looked at Euan for approval. "If that's alright with you?"

Euan only had to look at Lexie's face to know he couldn't stop the young man calling for her even if he wanted to, which he didn't.

After pouring Euan a cup of tea, Lexie went back to the task of soup making.

"So, if Charlie Mathieson didn't sent you that note, then who did?" Euan asked, his policeman's nature not liking a mystery.

Lexie shrugged her shoulders, no longer caring about anything other than next Saturday night.

"Have you still got it, the note I mean?"

Lexie nodded. "I think so."

"Let's have a look at it then."

Lexie found it in the pocket of the coat she'd been wearing that night and handed it to Euan, who carefully unfolded it and read the scribbled missive. This hadn't been written by anyone with a good education, he mused, noting the bad spelling and the ragged edge of the paper, which had obviously been torn from some sort of jotter.

He re-folded the note and slipped it into his shirt pocket. Annie gave him a questioning look, but Lexie had forgotten about it already, as she stirred the soup and daydreamed of Charlie Mathieson.

After tea had been eaten and everything cleared away, Annie brought the subject of the note up again. "Why are you keeping it?" she asked.

Euan took a deep breath. "Do you remember Robbie Robertson?" he said.

Annie nodded. "But that was a while ago now, what's he got to do with this, apart from happening to go by Lexie last Saturday...?" But even as she said it, she too became suspicious. "You don't think Robbie Robertson had something to do with this do you?"

"Maybe," Euan replied, "maybe not. But it does seem a bit of a coincidence that he turned up when he did and, this note," he unfolded it and handed it to Annie, "I think has the meaty hand of Robbie Robertson written all over it."

Annie looked closer at the page. "This looks like a page from the book Harry Duncan uses to write the butcher meat orders in." Their eyes met.

"Are you sure, Annie?"

She looked closely at the paper again. "Well, I can't be absolutely certain, but it does look like it."

She handed the note back to Euan.

"What are you going to do?" she asked, willing Euan not to upset the applecart that was her now happy daughter.

"I'm going to find out the truth," Euan stated. "I've already had words with that young man regarding Lexie and that silly engagement ring he gave her and I thought that that talking to had been enough, but perhaps another visit is needed."

Robbie was still preening about the trick he'd pulled on Lexie when Euan, in full sergeant's uniform, came into the shop.

Harry Duncan was quick to acknowledge the 'important' customer who was looking down at him from over the counter.

"Sergeant MacPherson," he smiled, "and what can we get you today?"

Euan glanced into the back shop where Robbie Robertson was now skulking, waves of panic gripping him at the sight of the 'long arm of the law'.

"I'd like to order some beef for the weekend," he said amiably. "We're having a bit of a celebration then, our daughter Lexie is bringing her new young man to the house to visit."

Robbie felt his blood run cold.

"Certainly Mr MacPherson," he replied, "I'll just fetch the order book."

Robbie tried to reason out how the policeman could have possibly found out about what he'd done and the cold in his blood suddenly began to burn as he waited while Harry Duncan produced the book, his pencil poised to write down the sergeant's requirements.

It was at this point that Euan produced the note from his tunic pocket.

"Do you have a page missing from you book, by any chance?" he asked the butcher casually.

In an instant Robbie knew, the game was up and he could feel the full weight of the law descending onto his shoulders. There was no escape as his boss turned back the pages of the order book and Euan matched the torn edge against the note.

"Looks like someone's torn one of your pages out," he stated matter-of-factly.

"ROBBIE!" the butcher shouted into the back shop. "What have you been up to?" But Robbie wasn't there. Total fear had overcome him and he had run out of the butcher's as fast as his legs could carry him, never to go back to Harry Duncan's shop again. Nor, he vowed, go within a thousand miles of Lexie Melville.

Euan smiled to himself. That was the last time Robbie Robertson would bother Lexie, he was sure of that.

"Actually," he turned to Harry Duncan, "as well as the beef, add in a pound of pork sausages and perhaps a half a dozen slices of that smoked bacon of yours for Sunday breakfast. Annie and Lexie's appetites have been a bit jaded of late, but I'm sure they'll feel more like eating by then."

Chapter 27

Annie and her family were getting ready for the coming christening of Nancy and Billy's new baby daughter. She had been born four weeks early and weighed in at six pounds, two ounces, with all fingers and toes intact. Nancy had checked, she said.

The baby had Mary's dark colouring with a crown of black hair, and her dad's nose and mouth and everyone agreed, she was the most beautiful baby ever born, especially her mum and dad.

Annie was to be her godmother and she was to be called Mary Anne Donnelly.

Lexie was searching through the chest of drawers in her room to find the jumper that Annie had knitted for her, when the letterbox rattled and the postman pushed a cream envelope through the door.

"I'll get it," called Lexie, holding the jumper up in front of her.

It was addressed to her mother and she ran through to the kitchen with it. "It's for you," she said, tossing the envelope onto the sideboard before drawing Annie's attention to the red jumper.

"This is lovely, Mum," she said. "You must teach me to knit like you, then I could knit a cardigan for Charlie," she decided triumphantly.

Annie smiled. It would be a long time before Lexie would have the patience to sit quietly and knit, but she didn't discourage her.

"Is Charlie coming with us tomorrow to the christening?" she asked. He had become quite a part of the family over the weeks since that fateful

Saturday and Annie had high hopes that the two of them would marry.

"Wouldn't miss it for the world," she said. "He really likes Nancy's husband, says he's the brother he never had. But I just think he likes to be part of the family, being an 'only one' like he is."

"Well, when you see him tonight, remind him it's at eleven o'clock at the Wishart Church so he'll need to be here at ten."

"OK Mum." And with that Lexie retreated to her bedroom and the mirror.

The cream envelope looked important and it was postmarked Belfast.

Annie only knew Bella from the old country, and this wasn't her writing, nor the kind of envelope she could afford.

She placed it on the table, balanced against the sugar bowl while she made herself some tea, glancing at it from time to time, a growing concern forming in her stomach that something had happened to Bella and the nuns were writing to let her know.

She could hear Ian and Lexie mumbling and giggling in the background, then the kettle started to whistle. She turned off the gas.

Forgetting about the tea, she picked up the vegetable knife, using it to slit open the envelope cleanly. Two pages of writing paper unfolded and a photograph of a young man fell out onto the table. Annie felt that her heart would stop beating as she gazed at the photograph of a young Billy Dawson. Only it wasn't Billy Dawson.

With trembling hands, she picked up the pages and began to read the neat slanting script.

Dear Miss Pepper,

My name is Dr David Adams and enclosed is a photograph of my son, John.

You may ask why I am writing to you, but John turned 18 in June of this year and my wife and I felt it was our duty to tell him that he was adopted and that his birth mother was yourself, Miss Pepper.

When she realised that we had spoken to John, your friend and our housemaid, Bella, told us she has been in touch with you over the years and that you were aware of John's adoption, so I want you to know that he has been very happy living with us and is about to go to University in Belfast, to also learn to become a doctor.

We are aware that your circumstances have changed and that you have a family of your own in Scotland, but John has asked if it would be possible for you to write to him sometime and get to know him. We are happy for this to happen, but it is entirely up to you, Miss Pepper. He also has no knowledge of who his real father is and, again, this is something I would leave you to decide whether or not to reveal to John, that is if you even know where the man is.

I will close now, I hope this letter has not been too much of a shock to you and I await your response.

Yours very sincerely.

Annie sat in complete silence, staring at the words and the photograph of her son.

Billy Dawson and Annie Pepper had produced this handsome young man. Out of lust or misguided love down by the river that day, as the flax harvest was being gathered in. The likeness to Billy Dawson was overwhelming, everything from John's black hair and eyes to his tall frame was the image of Billy Dawson, and Annie felt a huge surge of love for her son.

Of course he could write to her, get to know her and get to know his father too, if that's what he wanted. But that would mean telling Billy, she realised, and the thought filled her heart with confusion.

"Is everything alright Mum?" Lexie was standing by the kitchen door watching her, sensing that whatever was in the letter had disturbed her.

Annie quickly gathered the letter and photograph and pushed it into her apron pocket. "Everything's fine Lexie," she responded a bit breathlessly, "just fine."

She looked at the kitchen clock. "Goodness!" she exclaimed. "Look at the time. Your father will be home soon and I haven't even started on the tea."

Lexie frowned. Something had changed about her mother and it was something in that letter that had upset her.

"Do you want me to help?" she asked, but Annie bustled her out of the door.

"What I want you to do," she said, gathering her emotions back in, "is to go over to Sarah's and make sure everyone knows the time of the christening tomorrow."

"But," Lexie began.

"No buts, just do as I ask."

Reluctantly, Lexie did as she was bid, but was more certain than ever that something was wrong.

Sunday morning dawned bright and clear and Annie could hear Euan cooking the enormous breakfast he'd promised them all, to get them set for the christening, he'd said, especially for Annie who was to be Mary Anne's godmother alongside Billy Dawson as the child's godfather.

The smell of bacon and sausages seemed to fill the whole house and Ian and Lexie were already tumbling through to the kitchen ready for the feast. After a restless night's sleep, Annie's appetite had deserted her, but, somehow, she would force something down, blaming the nerves about being a godmother for her reduction in quantity.

"It's lovely," she told Euan, "I'm just a bit anxious about the christening, that's all."

Again, Lexie eyed her mother. "Did you tell Dad about the letter?" she asked, leaning forward so she could see Annie's reaction.

Euan took his place at the table, his plate piled high with Harry Duncan's produce.

"What letter's this then?"

Annie felt her stomach seize. "Oh that," she forced a smile at Lexie, "just a reply from Bella," she said, "remember I wrote to her a little while ago."

Lexie's eyes narrowed with doubt, but Euan accepted Annie's answer and tucked back into his breakfast.

The Wishart Church was already filling up with friends and well-wishers as Annie and her family arrived. The ladies had decorated the pews with flowers and ribbons and the organ was playing softly in the background.

"It's beautiful," Annie exclaimed, looking round for Nancy and the baby.

"Mr and Mrs Dawson paid for it all," explained Lexie, knowledgably, "Sarah told me, and there's tea and sandwiches and christening cake in the hall afterwards."

Annie gazed at her daughter. All of a sudden, Annie felt like the child with Lexie becoming the adult.

"Charlie and me will be sitting in the front row with Dad and Ian, so we can see everything," she continued, her voice becoming more bossy than usual, "and you'll be there," she ended, pointing to a place beside the font, "as Mary Anne's godmother."

Annie and Euan exchanged glances, their daughter was certainly growing up fast and Annie appreciated the diversion, as the rest of Nancy and Billy's family took their places. Annie did as she was told and stood at the side aisle ready to take her place.

Agnes and Charlie Cassiday, with Joe's three boys, sat a few rows back. Agnes was looking quite neat and tidy and Annie knew that Charlie had something to do with the transformation. She'd finally forgiven Nancy, who in turn had apologised for upsetting her the way she had and there was even talk of offers to babysit. Mr and Mrs Donnelly sat in the pew behind Annie's and clutched the pew bibles to hide their discomfort at being in a Protestant Church.

Josie Dawson, with her daughters Sarah, Elizabeth and Jane filed in and took their seats on the other side of the aisle, Josie acknowledging Annie with a smile and a small wave.

The murmurs of the congregation diminished as the Minister came out of the vestry and took up his place behind the font. He was followed by Nancy, carrying Mary Anne and supported by Billy who stood to the left of the font and finally, Billy Dawson entered, taking his place alongside Annie.

The sermon began, a hymn was sung and prayers for the baby and her parents were said and, finally, the Minister took Mary Anne in his arms and anointed her in the name of the Father, the Son and the Holy Spirit. Annie's eyes were misting over with the beauty of the moment when she felt Billy Dawson's hand brush against hers.

It was only for a moment and could have been by accident, but it sent a rush of heat through Annie that she'd not felt in a long time. Seconds later, it happened again, but this time his hand stayed touching hers.

The organ was playing somewhere in the distance and people had begun filing through to the hall for their tea. Mr and Mrs Donnelly were beaming at Mary Anne and Euan was gathering their brood together, but the only thing Annie was aware of was Billy Dawson's hand against hers.

Josie Dawson's voice seemed to come from nowhere.

"What a lovely service," she said to Annie, closing in on her, but her eyes were on her husband and she wasted no time in claiming him.

Annie felt the colour rush to her cheeks, as Josie linked her arm through Billy's.

"Shall we?" she nodded towards the door leading to the adjoining hall.

Without looking at Annie, Billy and his hand were gone.

It was the insistent voice of Lexie that brought Annie back to earth. "C'mon," she urged, "all the christening cake will be gone if we don't hurry."

Annie hurriedly forced a smile as she tried to quieten her racing heartbeat. What had just happened there? And why did it have such an effect on her, after all these years? Questions with no answers were scrambling through her head as she followed Lexie through to where Euan, Ian, and Charlie Mathieson were wading their way through a mountain of sandwiches.

"Lovely service," Euan mumbled, his mouth full, "and as for these sandwiches..." he looked around him till he caught the eye of Billy Dawson. "Thank you," he mouthed, holding up a triangle of bread and tinned salmon.

Annie dared not look up. Too much was happening in her heart and head that she needed to escape, be alone for a while, think this thing through. To have received the letter about her son only yesterday and to react, as she had, to Billy Dawson's touch today was almost too much for her.

She tugged the sleeve of her husband's jacket. "I'm feeling a bit unwell," she began. "Would you mind if I went outside for some fresh air? Maybe a bit of a walk would help." Euan put his sandwich down, concern filling his eyes.

"I'll come with you," he offered immediately, "Lexie and Charlie can see to it that Ian gets home alright."

"No, please, Euan, stay with them, then I'll know they'll get home safely. I just need some time on my own to settle down after all the excitement today..." She squeezed her husband's arm. "Please?"

Euan hesitated. Lexie had spoken to him about the letter which she was sure hadn't been from Bella, but contained bad news. Maybe Annie needed to grieve about something, he decided, she'd tell him in her own good time, he was sure of that. Sometimes one just needs to be alone, he reasoned, even if that someone was his wife.

"I'll see you back home then," Euan said quietly. Annie nodded, kissed him lightly on the cheek and walked away.

A cooling breeze had got up and helped fan the heat out of Annie's face as she walked down King Street and into the Murraygate. All the shops were closed and people in their Sunday best were going home from the many churches in Dundee, home to their families and loved ones who shared their lives and often meagre possessions.

Further and further she walked, till she came to the Magdelane Green, a grassy bank, which overlooked the River Tay.

It was here she had encountered Joe Cassiday while walking Nancy in her pram all these years ago. He was so handsome and full of fun then, and it was hard to believe that the little girl she'd pushed along the road that day would later become the death of him.

She sat down on a wooden bench and gazed out at the scene. It was Mary who had brought her to Dundee and it was Billy Dawson that had almost broken her spirit. The war had changed him, as it had everyone, but somewhere inside him she could still sense the spark of the young man he had been when she fell in love with him.

She opened her handbag and retrieved the letter and photograph, reading the words again and finally allowing her heart to settle on the picture of her son, her and Billy's son.

How different would life have been if it had been she who followed him to Scotland and not Mary? She would have become Mrs Billy Dawson and their son would have grown up knowing his real father and mother. *If only I could turn the clock back*, she thought sadly. *If only.*

It was becoming cold now, as the sun dipped behind some clouds and Annie's thoughts turned to Euan and Lexie, her daughter to Alex Melville and young Ian her son with Euan. She folded up the letter and returned it, along with the photograph to the envelope.

How could she tell Euan about her past? And Lexie, what would she say about a mother who had borne a child out of wedlock? A bastard, she'd call it. And there was Billy and Josie and their three daughters. Could she really destroy their lives by letting Billy know about his son? Were her feelings for Billy still so strong that she would jeopardise the happiness of so many lives to satisfy them?

She stood up to go, taking one last look at the river, forever changing from steel grey to silver as it moved through the days. *Nothing stays the same*, she thought, *but there are some things that must remain hidden and can only be revealed when the time is right. And that time isn't now.*

She took a deep breath. Maybe one day, Billy would know about their son and John would be able to know his mother, Annie Pepper. She smiled at the name, in the letter Dr Adams had called her by that name, but Annie Pepper was no more, she was now Annie MacPherson and proud to be so.

Yes, Annie decided, timing was everything and right now, it was time for her to go home to Euan.

THE END

10735655R00088

Printed in Great Britain
by Amazon.co.uk, Ltd.,
Marston Gate.